Shimmy for Me

A
California Belly Dance Romance
Novella

Book 1

Shimmy for Me

A
California Belly Dance Romance
Novella

Book 1

DEANNA CAMERON

Fine Skylark Media
California

Fine Skylark Media
P.O. Box 1505
Lake Forest, California 92609-1505

Shimmy for Me
Copyright © 2014 DeAnna Cameron
ISBN-13: 978-0-9908146-1-0 (print)
ISBN-13: 978-0-9908146-0-3 (ebook)

Cover by Sommer Stein, Perfect Pear Creative Covers
Cover photography by Valua Vitaly and Denys Kurbatov via Dreamstime

TITLES BY DEANNA CAMERON

THE DANCER CHRONICLES
The Girl on the Midway Stage
The Girl on the Vaudeville Stage

CALIFORNIA BELLY DANCE ROMANCE
Shimmy for Me
Dance with Me
Another Dance
Jingly Bells

PRAISE FOR *SHIMMY FOR ME*

"DeAnna Cameron delivers satisfying happily ever afters that will leave you sighing."

—Beth Yarnall,
author of *Wake Up Maggie*

"*Shimmy for Me* is a fantastic contemporary romance! … interesting entanglements that will leave the reader smiling."

—Sarah E. Bradley,
Ind'tale Magazine

PRAISE FOR *THE GIRL ON THE MIDWAY STAGE* (formerly *THE BELLY DANCER*)

"The characters in this novel will dance right off the page and into your imagination!"

—Brenda Rickman Vantrease,
author of *The Illuminator*

"A beautifully written page-turner with characters that leap off the page, *The Belly Dancer* transports readers into an exotic and sensual world within a world, as plucky but initially naive Dora Chambers fights Chicago society's conventions and her husband's indifference to discover, in the thrall of the Egyptian Theatre, a passion beyond her wildest dreams."
—Lynette Brasfield,
author of *Nature Lessons: A Novel*

"The 1893 World's Fair was a marvel, and in her debut, Cameron uses this backdrop to demonstrate one woman's view of herself. Society is forever altered because of what she learns in the lush, sensual, and exotic world of belly dancers. With a strong and vibrant picture of the era and a feminist approach to history, Cameron makes statements about women's rights and society's constraints."
—RT Book Reviews (4 stars)

PRAISE FOR *THE GIRL ON THE VAUDEVILLE STAGE* (formerly *DANCING AT THE CHANCE)*

"Old New York comes to vibrant life in this dazzling tale of follies and illusions. *Dancing at The Chance* serves up a racy, exuberant feast for the senses, with a lively and intrepid heroine determined to succeed in a fading world threatened by fast-paced, fickle modernity."
—C.W. Gortner,
author of *The Confessions of Catherine de Medici*

DEDICATION

To the belly dancers of the world for keeping this
beautiful and inspiring dance form alive.

CHAPTER ONE

"IT'S ONLY SEX," Abby Anderson said, keeping her focus on the mirror propped on the desk in front of her and the black eyeliner wand in her hand.

In the corner, Melanie flipped through a tattoo magazine. "It's about time. How you managed to go a whole year is a mystery to me."

"It's not like I planned it. It just happened. I've been busy."

Busy working two jobs—three if you counted the belly dance studio that was consuming every spare minute and dollar she had. It didn't seem possible that so much time had passed since her ex had given her the ultimatum: him or the studio. He didn't understand how she could leave graduate school and the prospect of a comfortable career to devote herself to what he considered a dead-end business. That's when she knew he didn't understand her—and he never would.

Most days, she was too busy to think about her wreck of a love life. Today she could think of little else.

May 1. Seeing the date on the calendar had brought it all back. That last terrible fight. All the awful things he'd said to her. She knew they weren't true. Pursuing her passion didn't make her selfish. It didn't mean she was damaged goods.

She'd find love again. Eventually. But tonight it wasn't love she was after. She just wanted to think about something besides that brain-dead temp job at the newspaper, the skimpy dance tips she earned at the restaurant, and the studio that sank her deeper into debt every day, even if it was the only thing that could still make her smile.

She wanted to remember how it felt to be touched. To feel lips pressed to hers, hands on her waist, maybe a caress or two. All the belly dance writhing and grinding in the world wouldn't scratch that itch.

She needed a man.

"Do you have someone in mind?" Melanie asked, distracted by the full-page photograph of a dragon tattoo she was holding beside her miniskirt-exposed thigh.

"No one in particular." Abby smoothed a thick layer of smoky eye powder over her lids with her fingertip, then double-checked the crimson silk blooms and rustic Middle Eastern pendants pinned to the scarf knotted around her head, leaving her thick batch of braids, leather strands, and long pheasant feathers to hang freely over her shoulder. She tucked in a few extra hairpins, then turned around. "Maybe that guy at the window table who always slips me his phone number with his one-dollar tip."

"Are you serious? He's got to be ninety years old."

Abby chuckled. "I know. I'm kidding. There's never a shortage of flirts hoping to score with the belly dancer, though. I usually ignore them, but tonight, who knows? Can you help me with my straps?"

Abby turned her bare back to her friend, who set aside her magazine to untie the halter's plum-colored straps. She tugged them tighter.

"Good?" Melanie asked.

"No. More." Abby squeezed the sides of her top, which consisted of more old coins and cowrie shells than fabric, until cleavage filled the deep V of her neckline.

Melanie tied the knot, inspected the front, and nodded. "Nice," she said. "The costume looks great with the tattoo."

Abby's fingers brushed the inked swoops and swirls that curved around her belly and disappeared beneath the waistband of the low-riding harem pants and all the belts, scarves, and tassels tied around her hips. The tattoo—a belated birthday gift from Melanie—was already two weeks old, but still sensitive to the touch. "It is nice, isn't it? Tell your boyfriend he does good work."

"No way," Melanie said. "It would totally go to his head. He's already impossible."

A pounding on the door interrupted them. "Two minutes," said a deep, accented voice.

"Okay, that's my cue to leave," Melanie said. "I've got to get on the road anyway if I'm going to get to

Hollywood before the show. The 405 will be a parking lot if I don't get moving." She pulled out her key ring, detached one of the keys, and set it on the desk. "Thanks again for letting me get some practice in at the studio. I locked it up. Oh."

Abby stopped dabbing at the color on her lips. She knew that tone.

Melanie pulled a folded piece of pink paper from her purse. "This was taped to the studio's door when I got there."

Abby took it. "Past Due: Warning" was stamped in thick black letters across the top. Her gut clenched. She wasn't surprised, but that didn't make it any easier. She pushed the paper into her bag. She wasn't going to think about it tonight.

Melanie bit her lip.

"It's nothing," Abby said, forcing a smile. "It's already taken care of."

"Really?" Melanie asked, cautiously. "Because if it isn't, if you need help—"

"I don't need help," Abby said. "Honestly. It's fine."

The last thing she needed was pity.

Two angry thumps on the door.

"Okay, I'm really leaving now." Melanie leaned over and kissed Abby's cheek.

"See you tomorrow." Abby watched her friend leave, then reached into her bag. No. She let go of the paper and pushed the bag away. Forget about the notice. Forget about the studio. Forget about her ex and the cold bed she crawled into every night.

Focus on tonight.

Abby looked into the mirror.

Zenina looked back. Part tribal belly dancer, part vaudeville chorine, part silent picture vixen. She had drawn from each of her favorite inspirations to create her performance persona. Her alter ego. Her dance self.

Three angrier thumps rattled the door.

"I'm coming," she hollered. This was it.

Three hundred and sixty-five frigging days. It was a long time. Too long.

"You can do this," she whispered to her other self. "It'll be just like any other performance." *Only better.*

By the time she took her place on the small stage, the lights were low, and a slow, snaky melody had filled the restaurant's main room. She was only a silhouette to the roomful of diners, holding her pose like a living statue. She usually closed her eyes during this prelude and focused on the energy of the music and the audience.

Not tonight.

In the darkness, her gaze roamed. She wanted a good view before the stage lights came up to brighten her, and blind her.

Nearly every seat was filled. A good draw for a Thursday night. Mostly couples, some groups. But it was the single men she searched for. The ones who sat on the fringe to watch.

Would it be the college jock tipping back beer in a bottle? The shy guy in the Oxford shirt fidgeting with his soda straw? Maybe the older . . .

A Suit at the bar caught her eye. One hand wrapped around a highball glass, the other tugging at his tie. Calm. Confident. And sexy as hell. The way his gaze locked on her made her tingle in all the right places.

He was the one.

CHAPTER TWO

DEREK COLLIER SIPPED his Macallan 18 and watched the restaurant's belly dancer come alive to the hypnotic rhythm pulsing through the dining room. When he'd seen the words "belly dancing" glowing in blue neon beneath the Sultan's Tent sign, he'd expected the kind of flashy beads and sequins dancer he'd seen a hundred times before.

He didn't expect this.

The poster at the front called her Zenina, a tribal fusion belly dancer. Whatever that was. From his vantage point at the bar, she looked like nothing he'd ever seen—part bohemian waif, part harem fantasy, part . . . Damn, the way she swayed and writhed up there was making it impossible to think.

It was a welcome diversion. Tonight, thinking was the last thing he wanted to do. He sipped again and felt the ice-chilled scotch pushing away the memory of the last five hours. The rage, the frustration, the betrayal. Six years he'd been away, and six years he'd been dreaming of the day he'd be back. Hell, he'd been dreaming of this his whole life. Working for it, preparing for it. And now . . . what did it matter? It was out of his hands. His father had made that clear. He wasn't going to make peace with it tonight—he couldn't imagine he ever would—so what was the point of sulking when there was something so much more interesting on that stage?

He stared hard at that amazing creature. At those milky white arms moving with a ballerina's grace. At those shaking hips. At that swirl of a tattoo around her middle, twisting and beckoning. He'd never seen anything like her before. He tugged on the Windsor knot at his throat. The scotch had to be working its magic because all he wanted to do was run his fingers along that tattoo. To trace the delicate lines on that soft, supple surface.

He drank again and welcomed the burn, but it did nothing to lessen the pulsing beneath his belt.

He turned back to the bar. He should probably mind his manners tonight. There were plenty of good reasons to behave himself. He still had a job to do. And he was still a Collier, for whatever that was worth. He raked his fingers through his hair in the way that made the short dark strands stand tall. He caught a glimpse of himself in the mirror behind the bar, then a flash of plum and silver caught his eye. A blur of seductive movement.

The belly dancer had left the stage and was dancing between the tables. He watched her dip backward, her spine nearly parallel to the floor. Her belly pulsed and fluttered, making the tattoo lines twitch and tease. God, she was limber.

His mind reeled with the possibilities when her dark-as-night eyes met his. Her hint of a smile made him weak in the knees. When she shimmied down the aisle in his direction, he had to remind himself to breathe.

Finally, when she stepped in front of him, it was all he could do to keep his hands to himself. Instead, he breathed in the warm scent of her, an intoxicating blend of flowers and spice. He wanted so badly to touch that long and lean torso, that tattoo so close he could trace every winding line, if he dared.

His cheeks flamed and his chest tightened against his starched Armani shirt. When she met his glance again with hooded, bedroom eyes, he struggled to remain composed.

His fingers fumbled in the pocket beneath his lapel and pulled out a bill he squeezed between two fingers. He lifted it, enticing her closer.

Another hint of a smile told him she needed no enticement. She was watching him as intently as he watched her. When she neared, he angled to slide the bill beneath the snuggest of her belts. But at his reach, she swung her hip away. He should have known. It was a game every belly dancer played, and she played it well. Offering up a hip, then pulling it away when he made his move.

His desire made him as clumsy as a schoolboy. After he'd made three tries, she wiggled her finger, and shimmied those flawless shoulders, jiggling that exquisitely full chest, then turned away.

His heart sank. Was their game over?

But she stopped. The music reached a dramatic pause, and before he knew what was happening, she dipped into another deep, reclining pose.

Only this time, her head was practically in his lap.

Those long, thin braids, those thick strands of violet and magenta yarn, the leather straps and feathers draped beside him. He stared, awed by the exotic headdress of red silk flowers and the ancient-looking jewelry, but it was those beautiful chocolate brown eyes and kissably soft lips that mesmerized him.

So. Unbelievably. Close.

He would capture that mouth with his own, if he could just catch his breath. If he could just . . .

She whispered, so quietly only he could hear, "The courtyard next door. After the show."

Was it a question? Was it a demand? It didn't matter. He'd say yes to anything. He managed a nod.

With liquid grace, she righted herself and shimmied away. When she reached the center of the room, the music reached its climax. She struck a pose and caught the final note with a bow.

Then she was gone, disappearing into the dark, leaving only the applause behind.

If she was true to her word, he knew where she would be. Where he hoped she'd be.

He put away the tip the dancer never took and twitched his finger at the bartender, who was lingering with another patron on the far side of the counter.

"Is there a courtyard nearby?" he asked as he paid his bill, surprised by how eager he was for the answer.

"You mean the one next door with the Spanish fountain?" the young woman asked. "It's pretty spectacular. But you'd probably want to see it during the day for the best view."

Derek nodded, but he knew better.

If that dancer showed up as promised, the very best view would be there tonight.

And he sure as hell wasn't going to miss it.

CHAPTER THREE

ABBY TOOK HER time in the office she used as a dressing room. She wanted to feel everything. The anxious anticipation, the intoxicating thrill. It all coursed through her like an electric current, awakening every nerve and pushing aside every thought. Everything but the image of him. That perfectly chiseled, perfectly attentive, perfectly astonishing specimen of a man sitting alone at the bar. The expensive suit had caught her eye, but it was his smile that had drawn her in. The subtle grin that was almost a smirk. The expression said he was there to play. No strings. No expectations. No complications.

He was perfect.

Slowly, she retouched her makeup. Carefully, she adjusted her costume. She rechecked the ornaments in her hair, her belts, her tassels. Finally, when she had stretched out every one of her little tasks, she took the piano shawl from her hips and retied it around her shoulders, letting the ivory fringe spill over her bare skin as protection against the nighttime chill that settled along the Southern California coast, even after an unseasonably hot spring day.

When she couldn't wait another moment, she slipped out the back of the restaurant, deposited her performance bag in the trunk of her car, and made her way across the darkened parking lot. Her destination was the building that looked more like a palatial hacienda, with its stucco walls and rustic pergolas, than one of Newport Beach's most prestigious—and beautiful—office complexes.

She paused at the edge of the archway, beside a patch of white jasmine blooms glowing silver in the moonlight. At the center of the courtyard, a fountain rose a full ten feet, maybe more. At the top, gentle streams cascaded from beneath King Neptune's feet and descended two tiers to a lighted pool that cast its liquid turquoise shimmer on the surrounding palms and bougainvillea. The massive structure looked like it belonged in a historic Spanish plaza. With its gentle trickling and beautifully rendered figures and reliefs, it could always calm her uneasy mind.

But tonight it wasn't an uneasy mind that had lured her here.

A movement in the shadows caught her eye. A man rising from a bench. It was him, and he was running his fingers through his hair, just as he'd done at the bar. A nervous habit? Was the anticipation getting to him, too?

From the shadows she watched the way the blue light danced along the smooth planes of his cheeks, his jaw, his lips. He was gorgeous, clean-cut, and sophisticated, but there was something else, too. Something in that crooked grin she could see even here. Even now.

Around her, the night air hummed with the distant din of traffic and diners leaving the restaurant. Footsteps scraping on pavement and voices drifting over the fountain's splash. But no one came their way. The office windows above stood dark and empty. They were entirely alone.

Her leg brushed something leafy that gave her a start. Soft and gentle, like a lover's caress. She thought again of the way he had watched her dance, as if they were the only two people in that dining room. Fresh desire flooded over her. To feel a man's touch again. This man's touch. It had been so long. Her body ached for it. She could do this. She wanted this.

Just for tonight.

She stared until she had memorized the narrow arc of his brow, the hard angle of his chin, the sharp curve of his jaw. When she was sure she could recall them all on the coldest and loneliest nights, she pulled the shawl more tightly around her bare shoulders, stepped from the shadows, and spoke.

"So, you've come."

CHAPTER FOUR

DEREK SEARCHED THE darkness, and found the belly dancer standing at the gate.

"Don't be shy," he said. "I don't bite."

She crept into the fountain's blue glow, and the effect took his breath. She looked like something from another world—certainly something beyond his world, with its usual salon-tanned, gym-slimmed social climbers eager for a place beside the future heir to the Collier family fortune.

This dancer was a beauty, though not in the ordinary sense. There was nothing ordinary about her. Was she blond? Was she brunette? It was impossible to say with all those strings, straps, and ornaments in her hair.

It hardly mattered. It wasn't the wild headdress that had drawn him to this hidden jewel courtyard in the dead of night. It wasn't the tender brown gaze that brushed over him like velvet, or that scanty bohemian costume, with all its shells and coins and fringe, or even that tattoo his fingers still itched to explore.

It wasn't any one thing in particular. It was all of it. The sum of this woman's strange and wonderful parts. She was a puzzle and a thrill ride, wrapped into one. Something new and utterly different, and tonight that was perfect.

Tomorrow he would deal with his father and the newspaper. He would do what the family expected and play his role.

But that was tomorrow.

Tonight, he wanted no part of that world. Only one thing could divert his thoughts tonight, and she was standing in front of him, just out of reach.

He bridged the distance and touched her porcelain white chin.

"Is this all right?" he asked.

She covered his hand with her own and nuzzled into it.

"We seemed to have skipped the introductions," he said, his eyes locked on that smooth, soft cheek. "I suppose I have the advantage. I already know who you are, Zenina, so maybe I should tell you I'm—"

She stopped his mouth with a quick finger. "No names," she said, her chocolate eyes widening. "No numbers. Nothing. All right? Let's just enjoy tonight."

She didn't want to get to know him? Or force him to get to know her? No hoops to jump through, no empty promises to make?

She really was perfect.

She took his hand from her shoulder and guided it down the front of her, over the rise of her breast, the soft slope of her belly, the ridge of her belts and scarves.

His chest thudded at the feel of her. His mind froze.

She stopped his hand and pulled it away.

She purred, "Do we have a deal?"

"Oh yeah," he said, his heartbeat racing, his breath coming fast. "You can have whatever you want."

A slow, sexy smile crept across her face and she rose on her toes to whisper in his ear. "Just for tonight, handsome. Just one night."

CHAPTER FIVE

"SO HOW WAS the show?" Abby asked Melanie when her friend stopped by her cubicle the next day.

"Oh no, you don't get off that easy," Melanie said. "Did you do it?"

Abby kept her eyes on her computer screen and her fingers moving on the keyboard. "Do what?"

She knew Melanie hated when she played dumb, but this wasn't the time for that conversation. Her boss wanted his revenue report before lunch and somehow she had to squeeze four hours of work into two.

"C'mon," Melanie said. "You ignored my texts. Didn't return my calls. Now you won't even fill me in? Just tell me—you hooked up last night, didn't you?" She wiggled her ruthlessly tweezed eyebrows, making her rolled Bettie Page bangs dance.

Abby bit back a smile.

"You did," Melanie squealed. "I knew it. I mean, I'm not surprised. Who could turn down Zenina, the hottest, wildest belly dancer in Orange County? Next to me, of course."

"Melanie." Abby clenched her computer mouse like it was her best friend's throat.

Teasing about hookups was one thing. But announcing she was a belly dancer to the world—or at least anyone within earshot in the *Herald*'s accounts payable department—that crossed the line.

For four months, she'd worked to prove herself in this lousy temp job. To be professional and dependable, an asset to the company. Not that it was her dream job—not by a long shot—but she needed it. And she already knew what happened when people who knew nothing about Middle Eastern dance found out she was a belly dancer.

It had happened in graduate school. First the funny looks, then the whispers. The smirks and eye rolls. It became obvious pretty quickly that she was never going to live down whatever ill-conceived image her classmates had. Then her MBA adviser had suggested a private performance or two might help her grade-point average. That was the last straw.

She might not have quit the program if Madame Almira hadn't announced her decision to retire to Florida and sell her belly dance studio—the studio that was like Abby's second home. But owning and operating the studio herself had seemed like destiny.

Who knew destiny had such a mean sense of humor?

"I'm just kidding," Melanie said tenderly. She touched Abby's shoulder lightly. "No one heard me. No one's here. Everyone's already downstairs. I was sure of it before I said anything. I'd never sell out my shimmy sister. Honest. I've got your back."

Of course, Melanie had her back. She knew that. It was just this damn deadline getting to her.

"I did think some good sex would loosen you up, though," Melanie whispered. "Guess it wasn't that good."

Abby didn't say anything, but the sex had been better than good. Part of her wanted so badly to tell Melanie about the incredible night she'd spent with that amazing man. That executive-suite god with the chest and abs that could make a woman cry. Or at least whimper with desire.

When he had pulled his car around—a black-as-sin Maserati that purred with horsepower—she thought nothing could top the feel of that butter-soft leather. But once he closed the door of the small villa at the Newport Beach Bay Club & Resort and pulled her in for a long and deep kiss that sent her heartache packing, she'd known the Maserati was not going to be her favorite ride of the night.

He had been everything she had hoped he would be. A gentleman who tempted her with soft kisses and tender caresses. He took his time, letting her be the one to urge him to the bed. She had undressed him and guided the foreplay before working herself on top of him. In the nearly complete darkness of the room, they had communicated with touch instead of words. Their bodies pressed and played together in perfect unison, as if they had always known each other.

It wasn't until sometime after three in the morning that he had given in to his exhaustion and fallen asleep, her cradled beside him, both of them naked but for the scarf, straps and feathers still wrapped around her hair. Only the silk blooms and pendants had tumbled out of place.

Around four, she had sneaked away, dressing quickly and slipping out to avoid an awkward good-bye.

The taxi driver wasn't thrilled by the measly five-dollar fare to ferry her the mile and a half back to her car, but she didn't care. That night had been exactly what she'd needed. Even though she had to show up to work with two hours of sleep, she felt better than she had in weeks. No wonder Melanie could see right through her. And she would give Melanie the details—eventually.

Right now, it still felt like a wonderful dream, and she didn't want it to end just yet.

The boss's office door flew open, bringing her thoughts back to her report. Carl Deffner emerged, tugging on the decades-old brown suit jacket he wore only for meetings with the publisher.

"Damn," Melanie said under her breath, hiding her face from Deffner. "I thought he was downstairs."

Deffner held up his watch. "Ladies, what are you still doing here? The meeting started five minutes ago. Get down there."

"I was telling Abby the good news," Melanie said.

"Wh—?"

"Shh," Melanie said under her breath. "Go with it." To Deffner, she added, "I didn't think you'd mind. You said it wasn't important, just fifth-floor politics," referring to the publisher and top-level executives who occupied the building's highest floor.

"I'm sure that isn't what I said," he said.

As Deffner's executive assistant for the past couple of years, Melanie wasn't shy about pressing him for information, or speaking to him the same sassy way she spoke to everyone. Despite their occasionally prickly exchanges, they seemed to work well together. He had saved Melanie from the layoff list more than once, and he was the reason Abby had gotten this temporary job.

"And I don't care what you're talking about, it can wait until after the meeting. So get down there. Both of you. The guys upstairs notice who walks in late, and if things go south down the road, well, I think you can see where I'm going here."

Even the hint of a layoff was enough to light a fire under Abby.

"C'mon, Melanie. Honestly, sir," she said, standing up and making her way to the aisle. "I didn't know I was supposed to go. I'm just a temp."

Deffner grumbled something and hurried past them. At the elevator, he pressed the button and looked back. "C'mon, ladies, now."

When he was out of earshot, Abby grabbed Melanie's arm. "So what's the big secret?"

Melanie glanced at Deffner and seemed to read in his expression that she was on the brink of pissing him off. "It's good news, don't worry," she whispered. "I'll tell you after the meeting."

Deffner held the elevator for them, and then set a brisk pace through the first-floor lobby.

"Has it started?" Melanie asked Jeanine, the receptionist with the silver beehive she adorned every day with a bow to match her pastel polyester suit.

"A few minutes ago, dear."

Deffner double-timed his pace to the building's auditorium.

Inside, the publisher was at the lectern, speaking with gushing optimism about the first-quarter numbers in both ad revenue and circulation. Since she had spent the last several weeks transferring revenue data from an old database into a newer one, and had seen the first-quarter revenue numbers herself, she knew they were nowhere near those cited by the publisher.

She was leaning in to Melanie's ear to remark on it when the publisher switched topics. He gripped the sides of the lectern, and his voice slipped with emotion. He spoke of his years with the newspaper, of good times and bad, and all the amazing memories. But that it was time.

It was as if a puppeteer had yanked a string. Those sitting straightened in their seats. Abby and the others standing in the back leaned forward. No one breathed.

"It's been a privilege to lead this fine news organization for more than twenty years," Randall Collier said, "but we need a change. It's a different world today than it was on the morning in 1983 when I was handed the publishing reins from Rutherford C. Collier, my late father and this newspaper's founder. And just as I took those reins from my father, it is my honor today to announce that effective immediately, I am handing them over to my son Derek Rutherford Collier. Derek, will you come up here, son?"

A man in a perfectly tailored gray suit rose from the front row and walked to the lectern. There were audible gasps from many in the room, but no one was as stunned as Abby. And no one was as near to fainting as she was because that well-dressed, slick-haired young Collier, the one being slapped on the back by the publisher and who was looking into the crowd with the seriousness of a wartime general, was the man who had just given her the best sex of her life.

"What's wrong?" Melanie whispered.

Abby tried to whisper, but her throat was too dry. The room was suddenly unbearably hot. She couldn't breathe. Her pulse raced, and her heart thudded. It was a panic attack. She hadn't had one in years, not since her very first belly dance performance, but the feeling was unforgettable. She leaned against the wall, told herself the room wasn't spinning. The world wasn't ending.

"What?" Melanie mouthed again, watching her with wide-eyed concern.

Abby swallowed hard. "Last night. Him." She pointed to the stage.

Melanie's expression changed from worry to confusion . . . to amusement. "You hooked up with Collier's son?" she whispered.

Abby covered her face with her hands. If only she could rewind the last twelve hours. She took a deep breath, and then another. Maybe Melanie was right. Maybe this wasn't so bad. She just had to steer clear of him. It wasn't as if she moved in the same circles as the executives.

She'd just stick close to her desk. Keep her head down. And what was she thinking? A guy like that wasn't going to waste time thinking about her. He'd probably already forgotten about her. And it had been dark. She had been in costume. If he saw her walking the halls in her wool skirt and cardigan twin set, he'd never recognize her. Not a chance.

Finally, she could breathe.

"Guess I'll have to stay away from the executive floor," she whispered back to Melanie.

Melanie's lips disappeared into a thin line and she shook her head.

"What?" Abby asked.

Instinct told her it wasn't good.

Melanie took her elbow and led her to the door. "We have to talk. Now."

CHAPTER SIX

"I THOUGHT THIS would be good news," Melanie said, closing the door to the ladies' restroom back on the fourth floor and checking for feet under the stalls.

"That what would be good news?" Abby said. She was trying to stay calm. Trying not to freak out. Trying to effing *breathe*. Her imagination was reeling with worst-case scenarios. "Damn it, Melanie, tell me before I throw up."

Melanie sank her tush against the sink counter. "Okay, but remember, I thought I was doing you a favor. I thought it was a good thing—"

"Tell me!"

"All right. The good news is that a great permanent position came up this morning. Deffner asked me if I wanted it, because, well, it would be a step up. But I'm not interested. I'd have to give up my four-ten work weeks, and I'd have no time for practice—"

"Melanie! I swear to God, if you don't get to it, I'm going to scream."

"I told Deffner you'd be a perfect second choice and he agreed. You have an interview at three o' clock, but I think the job is pretty much yours if you want it. It has to be filled immediately."

Abby cocked her head and replayed the information in her head, searching for the problem. She couldn't find one. "Why did you think I'd be upset? It's what I've been hoping for."

Melanie swallowed hard. "The job is assistant to the publisher."

Abby dropped back against the cold tile wall. Derek's assistant. She closed her eyes. Of course. It was an awful trick, dangling this perfect job in front of her. But the answer was simple. "I can't take it. I'll decline. I'll say I'm happy where I am."

Easy come, easy go, right?

Melanie didn't seem to think so.

"I *can* decline, right?" Abby pressed.

"There's something else you should know," Melanie said, her cherry-red lips puckered in distress. "The departments have been told to cut back on nonessentials. Deffner has to make cuts, and your position is one that has to go."

"But the job is supposed to last till June. It's only May."

"I know. He thought it would take longer to input the old data into the new system. You're just a lot faster than he expected."

"You're kidding. I did so well that I worked myself out of a job?"

Melanie's expression crumpled. "I'm so sorry. I know it isn't fair. It's this stupid company. The rumor is there'll be more layoffs if they can't meet this quarter's numbers. It sucks."

Abby knew what that meant. Even if she managed to keep her job, a temporary employee would be the first to go if layoffs were announced. She might be hired back after the dust had settled, but it would be too late to save her studio. "I can't believe that hypocrite Collier was just down there boasting about the first quarter and how great the numbers looked."

"It's all morale bullshit," Melanie said. "You know it better than most. You've seen the real numbers."

She hadn't run the revenue and expense numbers side by side like a tax accountant, but moving all the financial data for the last ten years over to the new system had given her a window into what was coming in, and what was going out. The company was in the red—deep, bloody, painful red. It had been for months, and it was getting worse, not better. But only someone paying close attention would notice Randall Collier had quoted expense numbers collected after last year's layoffs, but revenues that were projected before the staff had been cut by a third. It was a smokescreen to make the rank and file feel like their sacrifices had been worth something, and that the cuts had been enough.

Clearly they weren't.

"So basically, I have no job?" She was still struggling to grasp it, but it was the absolute worst thing that could happen. The belly dancing gig at the Sultan's Tent helped, but the newspaper job paid the bills.

"You're overqualified for this job anyway," Melanie said. Trying to find a silver lining. "No one with an MBA from Chatham University should be tapping numbers into a database."

"I don't have an MBA. I have one year in the MBA program. That's it." That decision to leave early and take over the belly dance studio had seemed so much sounder then than it did now.

"Do you regret leaving?" Melanie asked.

"No." She didn't regret it. Even now, as hard as it was, she would do the same thing again. She thought of her father and how much he had sacrificed to get ahead in his brokerage firm. He put off everything that had made him happy, telling her there would be plenty of time for all that when he was retired. But he'd never reached that retirement. A late-stage pancreatic cancer diagnosis had seen to that. She didn't want to live that way. Dancing made her happy. It was her life, and that studio was her dream.

More than once she had thought that those dark days at Chatham, after her belly dance secret had gotten out, had been a blessing in disguise. That they had pushed her to the path she should have been on all along.

It had taken nearly every dollar she'd inherited from her father to buy the dance studio, but she had a good business plan. Although students loyal to Almira had dropped off, she knew they'd return when Abby proved she meant to continue the Shimmy Shop as a dedicated belly dance studio. And that wasn't all. She had bigger plans. One of the unfinished dance rooms would make a wonderful retail boutique one day, and that coupled with a large storage area in the back could support an online retail store, too. She also wanted to apply to the city to serve coffee and snacks, and turn the main dance room into Shimmy Café at night where students could practice their performance skills and locals could come in to enjoy the entertainment.

Once she got out from beneath all these business costs, there was no end to the possibilities. She just needed a little more time to catch up with the bills. And she needed this job to do it.

"You know, I went to that belly dance show in Hollywood last night," Melanie said. "It turns out it was a benefit. A dancer from Silver Lake was in a car accident, and she needs help paying her hospital bills."

"That's awful," Abby said and silently chastised herself for wallowing. No matter how bad her money problems were, they were still just money problems. Melanie was trying to remind her of that. "Is it someone we know?"

"I don't think you know her, but that's not my point. I was thinking you should consider holding a benefit for the studio. If people would help a dancer get back on her feet, why not a whole studio?"

"I appreciate the idea. It's probably a good one. But I don't know the first thing about holding a benefit. The rules, the laws. I'm sure there's a ton of red tape. I wish I had the time to look into it. I just don't."

"You're right," Melanie said. "It was a stupid idea."

Abby reached out for her friend's arm. "It wasn't a stupid idea. At all. I know you're trying to help me. It's just taking everything I have to tread water right now."

"There's always my other idea," Melanie suggested.

Abby recognized that mischievous look. She shook her head. "No way. Absolutely, no way."

"Oh, c'mon. Do you know how much those dancers make? As much as you make here in a whole week. And what's the harm?"

"It makes belly dancing look like a joke. People think it's just like sending a stripper."

"Bellygram dancers are not strippers. Well, most of them. Of course, you're going to have bad seeds out there doing whatever they want, but we could do it with style. We could make it classy."

It wasn't the first time Melanie had suggested the side business as a way to boost revenue at the studio. Abby was open to a lot of suggestions, but this one— no way. This is where she drew the line. "If it came to that, I think I'd rather lose the studio."

Melanie shrugged. "All right. You're the boss."

Abby tugged her elbow. "I appreciate it, though. I know you're trying to help."

"So what are you going to do?" Melanie said when she pulled away.

"The only thing I can do, I guess. I'm going to take that assistant job. What do you think he's going to do when I walk in and say, 'Hi, remember me? I'm the one whose nipples you were sucking last night.' "

Melanie's mouth dropped open. "Oh God, don't say that. If he's anything like his father, he probably doesn't have much of a sense of humor. You'll knock him on his country-club ass."

Abby's chest seized. She could feel the world pulling away from her again, tugging at everything she held dear. No, if she was going to lose everything, it wouldn't be because she just gave up. What she needed was a plan, and little by little one was beginning to form. "What if I don't say anything?"

"What do you mean?"

Abby wasn't sure exactly. She pinched her lower lip and began to pace, her kitten heels clicking against the tiled floor. "I was in my costume, right? Full makeup, hair braided and wrapped."

"Okay?"

"Except for the performance in the restaurant, he only saw me in the dark. Outside, then his car, then the hotel room." It was all replaying in her mind, every sensuous moment, and every one in the dark.

"You made him do it in the dark?" Melanie half scoffed, half chuckled.

Abby's lips spread into a slow, relieved smile. "You bet I did. So, how in the world could he think of the belly dancer he sexed last night when he gets a look at this." She turned to the restroom's full-length mirror and posed, relishing every inch of her pale-pink-cardigan, gray-wool-skirt, plain-Jane glory.

"That's a good point," Melanie said. "But just to be sure"—she tapped the sink—"wash your face. Without makeup—I mean, no liner, no lipstick, no blush, nothing—he'll never see a resemblance. I don't know if I'd recognize you."

The idea made sense. Abby smiled a suddenly hopeful and altogether wicked smile. "So, I can just act like nothing happened. Like we're complete strangers. I never even told him my real name."

"Damn," Melanie said. "This really could work. And from what I hear, he's kind of a playboy anyway. He's been traveling like crazy for years, working at different Collier Media papers. He spent a year in Odessa, a year in Billings. Geez, I don't know how many places. He's basically been a really big fish in a lot of really small ponds, and he's never been lonely. If you know what I mean."

"Great." It was, wasn't it? A one-night stand, that's what she wanted. No complications. It just felt odd to be wishing the guy she'd just slept with had already forgotten her. She yanked off the elastic hair band holding back her ponytail and shook out her hair, bringing it down alongside her cheeks. She pulled a comb from her purse, wet it and worked out the bend. It was still a little noticeable. She turned to Melanie. "What do you think?"

"Honestly? You look like a dork."

She pulled a paper towel from the dispenser, wiped off her lipstick, blush, and eye shadow, then pinched her cheeks to make them splotchy and red. "Do I look like Zenina?"

Melanie pulled back and shook her head. "Not even a little."

CHAPTER SEVEN

DEREK PACED IN front of his father's desk. "A little warning would have been nice."

Randall Collier slid back in his leather chair and laced his fingers behind his head. "It was a board decision, yesterday afternoon. You should have attended. You may be publisher, but you're also a board member. Don't forget that. Still, I would have discussed it with you last night, if you had come home."

Home? That sprawling mansion overlooking the Corona del Mar shoreline hadn't felt like home since he'd finished college six years ago and set off for the *Pocatello Times*, the first stop in his father's idea of an apprenticeship. Since then, Derek hadn't spent more than a handful of nights in that place, and now that he was back in Orange County for good, he knew he couldn't take up residence there again. Especially after yesterday's illuminating discussion with his father

about the future of the *Herald* and the rest of the
Collier Media Group. As soon as Derek had left their
lunch chat at Morton's, he had stopped by the
Newport Beach resort and booked a villa.

"You didn't really expect me to move back into
my old room, did you?" The staff had removed the
car posters and baseball memorabilia he had
surrounded himself with in his teens and replaced
them with more tasteful furnishings, but they couldn't
rid it of the memories. "It's time I find a place of my
own."

"Whatever you prefer. So long as you intend to
see this business through."

"If you mean, so long as I intend to show up
every day and pretend everything is fine, well, I guess
you've left me no other choice."

Randall Collier leaned forward and frowned.
"You're making too much of this. It isn't so bad. The
departments have been given their numbers. They're
already trimming expenses. Your job will be easy."

Derek stopped in front of the wall of windows
looking out over a corner of Santa Ana and on to
Costa Mesa, Newport Beach, and a shadow of
Catalina Island on the horizon. "Right, easy." And
temporary.

A soft knock at the door stopped him.

"Yes, Mildred?" Randall said.

The door opened and a small, birdlike woman
with a tight black bun poked in her head. "Your three
o'clock has arrived, sir."

Derek turned back from the window. "Mildred,
please tell me there is some way to persuade you to
reconsider? How will I survive without you?"

She dipped her head. "Don't be silly. You'll be fine. It's my time. I've worked for your father for so many years, you know. We have our little way of doing things. You kids today have your computers and your smartphones, and who knows what else." She batted the air as if shooing all that technology away. "You need someone who understands it all. Someone who can really help you. Besides, I've always wanted to see the village in Sicily where my mother was born. If I don't go now, I may never have a chance."

Derek walked up to her, took her hand and pressed it to his lips. "You know you've broken my heart, Mildred. I thought I would finally have you all to myself."

The woman pulled back and slapped him on the chest. "Derek Collier, you are a scoundrel." There was a smile on her lips.

"All right. Then if you won't have me, let's see who's going to be stuck with me."

A moment later, Mildred showed in a woman who looked more like an underage sorority girl than the overqualified MBA student that brown-noser Deffner had promised him. Maybe it was just as well. He wanted an assistant who was smart, but not too smart. If he was going to do this, he needed someone who followed directions and didn't ask a lot of questions.

"Good afternoon, Miss Anderson," Randall Collier said, rising from his desk and coming around to greet the young woman, who was standing in the center of the room with her hands clasped in front of her like a child summoned to the principal's office. "Won't you have a seat?"

She lowered herself to the edge of one of the leather chairs.

"This is my son, Derek," Randall Collier said as Derek came around to greet her.

She took his hand politely, but hardly met his glance.

"Pleasure," he said.

She mumbled something unintelligible.

Was she nervous? Probably. But who could tell with that dark curtain of hair obscuring her face? Otherwise she wasn't bad-looking. Petite and thin, a little shapeless for his taste. Not like that belly dancer. Now that woman had curves. And when she had wrapped her legs around him . . .

"You've been working in a temporary position in Carl Deffner's department, is that right?" Randall Collier offered, trying to fill in the silence.

For the hundredth time that day, Derek pushed the belly dancer from his mind. It was almost annoying, the way she kept popping into his thoughts. He had needed the distraction last night, and she had served her purpose. But now he needed to focus.

Even if this mousy accounting clerk had to be the subject of that focus.

"We understand you've made great strides with the new accounting software and getting our old information integrated. Deffner says we're a month ahead of schedule, thanks in large part to you."

She nodded.

Father was trying so damned hard to get this girl out of her shell, but she just sat there, hunched in her chair, raising her glance from the floor for a split second at a time.

"I've enjoyed the work," she said at last.

"I'm glad to hear that. Unfortunately, since the project has entered its final stages, Deffner says he no longer requires the extra help."

So that was the tack the old man was going to take. Dangle the threat of unemployment. Derek stifled a laugh. Was it really any surprise this company was in the pitiful shape it was in?

Derek watched Miss Anderson. Her expression gave away nothing. She was as calm and expressionless as Derek hoped he was himself.

Perhaps he had misjudged her. Maybe she wasn't scared. Maybe she was cautious. A shrewd observer. A listener. Someone like him.

"Is that why you called me up here, Mr. Collier?" she said matter-of-factly.

"A woman who gets down to business," Randall Collier said. "I like that."

Derek liked it, too.

"We believe in taking care of our own around here," the older Collier continued. "We want you to know we appreciate your hard work and dedication."

What a load of BS. Did his father really think the woman would believe that? It didn't matter. His father wasn't pausing for a reply.

"As you must have heard in the auditorium this morning, I've decided it's time to retire. I'm handing day-to-day operations over to Derek, and my secretary, Mildred, has decided it's her time to leave as well. Which leaves Derek in need of some help. Doesn't it, son?"

This whole thing was becoming annoying. It was ridiculous, the way his father was treating this woman. This wasn't 1960. Hell, no one even used the term "secretary" anymore.

Apparently he wasn't the only one losing patience, because Miss Anderson looked like she had had enough as well.

"Are you offering me an executive assistant position?" she asked.

Her direct question left his father speechless.

"Yes," Derek interjected. "We are. But there's something you should know before we go further."

"Perhaps this isn't the time," Randall Collier said.

"It's the perfect time," Derek countered, meeting his father's glare squarely. He turned back to the young woman. "Let me spell it out," he said. "This is a challenging time for the newspaper. I'm sure your clerical skills are adequate, and your business experience could be an exceptional benefit. But what I'm really looking for is someone I can trust. Can I trust you, Miss Anderson?"

CHAPTER EIGHT

ABBY GLANCED UP from the floor and made eye contact with Derek for the first time since entering the office. If she had been standing, the force of it would have knocked her on her ass. As it was, she swallowed hard and tried to forget how those wide, scrutinizing eyes had looked so warm and inviting in the moonlight. Here, in the harsh afternoon sunshine, she could see they were the cold gray-green of the ocean when it crashed and tumbled into a white froth against the shore.

"Miss Anderson?"

His frown betrayed his impatience, but he didn't seem to recognize her.

And she hardly recognized him. Where was the sweet, tender guy from the night before?

Concentrate. "You can trust me, Mr. Collier."

Remember why you're here. Remember the studio. Nothing else. Not the silvery moonlight glancing off his strong, smooth chest. Not the heat of his lips. The soft brush of his stubble or the touch of his . . .

Stop!

"Good," he said. He stood and walked to the window, his gaze climbing the foothills in the distance. "Because I'm about to tell you something that cannot leave this room."

"Derek," his father said sharply. He was on his feet, his fingers angry talons on his desk. "This isn't wise."

"I think it is. If she is to be my only accomplice in this, she won't be much use if she doesn't understand the risk."

"There's risk?" Abby asked.

"Yes, Miss Anderson, there is risk," Derek said. He paced from the window across the floor behind her, his hands clenched behind his back. "I'm sure you've heard the rumors. About the cuts. Despite what my father presented this morning"—he shot a disgusted look at his father, who met it with stony silence—"the paper is experiencing unprecedented and unrelenting losses. Instead of making real changes, the family has been subsidizing operation costs."

"Even after last year's layoffs?" she asked.

"Those across-the-board layoffs probably made the situation worse," Derek said.

Again she caught a frigid glare directed at his father. "The family has been propping up the paper for months now, and it doesn't look like the situation is going to improve any time soon. So, the Collier Media board members—my esteemed aunts and uncles who have grown used to a steady stream of profits—have decided it's time to sell."

"Sell the paper?" she asked, stunned.

"All twelve papers," he answered. "And the radio stations. Everything."

Randall's leather cushion exhaled as he slumped back. "Really, Derek," he muttered, frustrated yet powerless.

"But you've just been appointed publisher," Abby said, struggling to process the revelation. "Why do that, if the paper's about to be sold?"

"Funny, I've asked the same question myself," Derek said. "It would seem my father and the rest of the board members believe the job requires someone with less attachment."

She could hear the sharp, prickly edges in his voice.

But the clamoring within her nearly drowned him out. She blurted the words thrumming within her. "If the paper is sold, what's going to happen to our jobs?" *What's going to happen to my job?*

He shrugged. "It depends. Several potential buyers have already expressed interest. Some, I imagine, would want to keep the company and all its parts intact. Others would probably break up the media group and resell the individual properties. As for the *Herald*, as long as it continues to publish, I believe most, if not all, of the staff would be retained. You and I, however, would not. Any buyer would naturally want to install a new publisher. Since I would be let go, it is a fair assumption that you, as my assistant, would be let go as well." He turned back to his father, who was slumped and distraught, and looking much less like the executive titan he had appeared to be in the auditorium. "Do I have that right, Father?"

The old man nodded.

"So, that's the bad news," Derek said. "Here's the good news: If you agree to accept the position as my assistant, you will receive the customary salary for such a position—which I assure you is a good deal more than your current wages—as well as a ten-thousand-dollar bonus upon termination, which we'll call your severance package."

A raise and a ten-thousand-dollar bonus? She could finally catch up on the bills. She could pay them off and still have enough to launch the boutique and website. No more month-to-month. No more struggling.

Derek cocked his head to the side. "What do you say?"

Her answer was clear. "How soon can I start?"

CHAPTER NINE

ABBY ARRIVED EARLY for the Friday night show and took her time getting ready in the office. Slipping into her costume, doing her hair, applying makeup—it was a welcome return to something normal after a day that had been anything but.

At least it had ended well, with a better paying job and the prospect of a bonus that could finally free her from needing a day job at all.

It should have been a dream come true.

It *was* a dream come true.

So why did she feel sick to her stomach?

Zenina's dark, accusing glare stared back from the mirror.

"Don't look at me like that," she muttered, swabbing her sable brush against the smoke-colored eye shadow. "You would've done the same thing."

No, she wouldn't. Zenina was tougher. More confident. She wouldn't have been ashamed to face

the man she had just used for sex. She would have
faced that awkward moment head-on and put it
behind her.

Now it was too late. Abby had lied to Derek. She
had told him he could trust her, even as she was
deceiving him. There'd be no forgiveness if she came
clean now. The way he had glared at his father, the
way he had sneered. She could hardly expect anything
better.

It didn't matter if her stomach was twisted in
knots. She'd have to keep up the lie if she wanted to
keep her job. It was the only way she could save the
studio.

At least it wouldn't be for long. Just until the
paper sold.

Then she'd be free. Sweet liberation. That's what
she had to remember. Spending her days at the
studio, adding classes, building the boutique,
developing the website. All the things she had no time
to do now.

And of course she could dance.

The vise grip loosened around her chest. Maybe it
wouldn't be so bad. Derek hadn't recognized her.
Why would he? He had so many more important
things on his mind.

He had hardly looked at her during the meeting.
And if she had to guess, it would be the same when
she showed up on the fifth floor on Monday morning
ready to work.

The knock on the door reminded her it was time.
She checked her image in the mirror. From behind
her costume and her makeup, beneath the armful of
bangles and the headdress, she felt the surge of

Zenina's strength. The feeling that anything was possible.

The feeling carried her to the stage. When the music began, her mind was clear. Do the job. Get the bonus. Focus on the studio. Easy as that.

She was still grinding through the slow-tempo opening when he walked in and took the same seat at the bar. Wearing the suit he'd worn in the office. And the same grim expression.

Her gut twisted like a pretzel.

CHAPTER TEN

"Macallan," Derek said to the bartender. "With ice."

"You got it, boss." The man shot him with his thumb and forefinger.

Irritating.

Derek nodded and turned back to the stage. Christ, what was he doing here? She'd made it clear she didn't want to see him again. Hell, she'd left the villa without even saying good-bye. And it wasn't like he was in the habit of forcing himself on women. Even ones he couldn't get out of his thoughts.

So why was he here?

He hadn't planned to come. He'd left the office intending to stop by his father's house to pick up a few changes of clothes. Then maybe grab a burger and turn in early. Get some much-needed sleep after last night's marathon.

Last night. Damn, there they were again. Those images that had burned in his mind all day. Her gorgeous curves in the moonlight. That wild tattoo he'd traced with his fingertips along her hip, and around to the small of her back.

But it wasn't just her beauty that had surprised him. That woman was not only willing, but assertive. He'd never been with someone who knew exactly what she wanted and how to ask for it.

He'd been more than happy to oblige. Just the thought of her revved him up all over again.

But he had to be practical. This wasn't the time to start something. He had to focus on the newspaper. And his plan.

His father and the rest of the family had their ideas about what to do with the *Herald* and the rest of the Collier Media stations and papers, but he was coming up with a few of his own. He just needed time. If he played it right, he'd have what he needed before the month-end meeting, when the board planned to select a buyer.

There was a great deal to be done, so why had he turned left, when he should have turned right, and found himself here?

He drenched the question in another sip of cold scotch and glanced across the room.

It was her fault.

It was impossible to read her eyes beneath that heavy makeup and from this distance, but he was sure she wasn't happy to see him.

He'd been here fifteen minutes and there hadn't been a single coy glance. No flirtation.

Let her play that game. He had a game of his own. He reached into his breast pocket, pulled out a twenty, and held it high enough she couldn't miss it.

It worked. Barely. When she finally approached, she had pulled one of the fringed shawls from around her hips and cocooned her head and shoulders. It was an alluring effect, but he wanted to see her face.

He could remember the length of her legs and the delicate curve of her neck. The swell of her breasts and the tiny nipples that had become hard pebbles beneath his touch.

But her face was less distinct. It was a blur he wanted defined.

He ached to see that face.

Instead he saw her back, and that tattoo swaying with her gyrating hips. He was so focused on those hips he nearly missed it when she leaned back and whispered, "You shouldn't be here. We had a deal."

He tucked the bill into her belt. "I had to see you."

The song's tempo increased, pushing to a climax. The movement in her hips quickened, too. "I don't want to see you," she said over her shoulder.

Then she was gone, in long strides that took her back to the center of the dining room where she flung up one arm exactly as the song came to its end. She bowed, and vanished into a dark corridor to the sound of applause.

CHAPTER ELEVEN

ABBY SLAMMED THE office door behind her and dropped into a chair. Why was he here? They'd agreed. One night. That was it. If he saw her again, even in the restaurant's dim light, he'd recognize her and it would ruin everything.

And then that trick with the tip. If he hadn't made himself so obvious, she could have ignored him. But everyone had seen the way he'd waved that bill around. If she didn't collect it, what would the staff think? As it was, the bartender had noticed her strange behavior. The way he had watched her from behind the bar, he knew something was up. What if he said something to the manager?

She had to say something first.

She picked up the desk phone receiver and punched the bartender's extension.

"Marco," he barked in his typical clipped way.

She could hear the synthesized Middle Eastern music in the background.

"Hi, Marco. It's Zenina."

"Ah, yes. Red or white, my darling?"

Sometimes she finished her nightly performance with a plate of hummus, pita bread, and a glass of wine. Food and drink orders were about the only interaction she ever had with Marco.

"Nothing tonight. Actually, there was a guy at the bar."

She heard Marco chuckle. "Yes?"

"Is he still there?"

"Yes."

She sucked in her breath. This was bad.

"Does he look like he'll be leaving any time soon?"

"No."

"Damn." The word slipped out before she could stop herself. "I need to ask a favor. It's important."

"Okay." The syllables came slowly. He was already suspicious.

"He's becoming a problem. Tell him I don't want to see him. I never want to see him. Please make sure he leaves."

"Yeah, okay."

"Could you call me in the office when he's gone? If it's not too much trouble?"

Marco agreed. She knew this was an awful thing to do to Derek, but she couldn't face him. She couldn't risk him recognizing her. There was too much at stake.

When the phone rang, she was nearly out of her costume.

"He's gone," Marco said.

"How'd he take it?" She winced. She didn't care. She didn't.

"Hard to say."

What did that mean?

"But he's gone. You're good."

Good. She was good.

She didn't feel good.

"Thanks," she said and hung up.

She took her time packing everything back in her performance case. She changed out of her costume and into jeans and a sweater. She wouldn't get to the hair and the makeup until she was home, but she still managed to burn another ten minutes. Finally she built up the courage to leave.

CHAPTER TWELVE

ABBY STEPPED OUT into the night with her performance case trailing behind her. It was dark, even darker than usual because the bulb on the parking lot's single light pole was out, and the moon's Cheshire cat grin offered little illumination. Slowly, she made her way through the rows of parked cars till she reached her own, opened the trunk, and hoisted her rolling case inside.

The sounds of footsteps stopped her. She straightened and slid her hand into the front pocket of her jacket, fishing for her keys or anything she could use as a weapon.

The footsteps grew closer.

It could be someone leaving the restaurant. It could be anyone.

"Was it something I said?"

It was Derek.

She relaxed, but only a little.

He didn't sound angry, or drunk. He sounded . . . sad.

"No," she said, fighting the urge to turn around and comfort him.

Her fingers abandoned her keys but curled into fists in her pockets instead. "It was a great night," she said in a coarse whisper she hoped disguised her voice. "I just want to leave it at that."

She made for the driver's side door and got as far as opening it before he was beside her. His hand shot out, planting itself against the window to stop her, then he pulled it back.

"Don't leave," he said.

The plea nearly broke her resolve.

Where was the stern, stoic suit she had seen today? Where was that brusque, bordering on rude young executive he had been only a few hours ago?

This was the man who had sheltered her last night. Who had indulged her fantasies, taking her from one orgasm to another and another.

This was the man who had melted her heart.

She had to get away.

He touched her arm, and he must have sensed her hesitation. His fingers brushed over her shoulder, to her neck. With her back still to him, he couldn't see the way that simple gesture nearly undid her. She wanted to turn and bury her head against that strong, wide chest. She hated herself for wanting it, but she did. She wanted his shelter. She wanted to beg his forgiveness. She wanted to throw herself on his mercy.

He stroked her neck, and her body remembered all the wonderful things he had done to her the night before.

"I don't want one night," he whispered.

If he only had said those words last night. Before everything was on the line. Before everything was so complicated.

"I want to know you, Zenina."

But she wasn't Zenina. Not even close.

She broke free from him and slid into her driver's seat.

"Please leave me alone," she said before slamming the door. Somehow she managed to turn the key and start the car.

The last thing she saw as she pulled away was him, watching her leave.

CHAPTER THIRTEEN

TWO NEW STUDENTS showed up for the Saturday morning belly dance class, but Abby still couldn't shake her mood.

Melanie approached her during the water break. "Are you all right?"

"I'm fine," Abby snapped and instantly regretted it. "I'm sorry. I didn't mean that. It's just been a strange couple of days."

Melanie glanced around, then leaned in close. "I saw the final notice on your desk."

Oh, yeah. There was that, too. Taped to the door this morning when she arrived.

"That raise is going to help, right?" Melanie asked. "If you need more, just say the word."

"No. They can't kick me out for another month, and by then I should be able to dig myself out of this hole."

She wanted so badly to tell Melanie the whole story. About the windfall that would land in her lap once the paper sold and the real reason Derek had been brought in as publisher. But she couldn't breathe a word about any of it. She couldn't make Melanie an accomplice in the deception.

All she could do was demand Melanie's job be protected when the paper sold. Derek had obliged. Any new owner would need a staff, he said. It was only the top-floor executives and their assistants who were likely to go.

"It must be weird," Melanie said.

"What?"

"Working for him. Being on guard all the time so he doesn't recognize you. I still think you're crazy for not telling him. He might even laugh about it."

Abby thought about the way he had leveled those cutting glances at his father. No, he wouldn't laugh about it.

"He came back to the restaurant last night."

"You're kidding," Melanie said. "What happened?"

"He ambushed me in the parking lot. Said he wanted more than a one-night stand."

Melanie jiggled her shoulders. "Left him wanting more, huh?"

"It's not funny."

"Okay. If you say so. But didn't he recognize you?"

"No. It was too dark, and I still had most of my makeup on."

Melanie stepped back and scrutinized her. "You like him, don't you?"

"No. Of course not."

"No one would blame you. He's gorgeous. He's rich."

Melanie stalled there, but Abby silently finished the list. He was also smart and thoughtful, gentle and considerate. Thinking back on that night, it wasn't just the way he had made her orgasm, but the moments when they had lain together, not talking, but comfortable in the silence. It was the warmth and the woodsy scent of him. The way he had kissed her forehead. The way he had fluffed her pillow. The way he had asked so many questions about her tattoo. When did she get it, why, had it hurt? She would have expected a man like him to disapprove of her ink. But he hadn't. When he kissed it, it felt like the most tender, intimate thing in the world.

Not that it mattered now. He was the only thing standing between her and keeping her studio.

"He'll be a good boss," she said, and tried to mean it. "If I don't screw it up."

"And if he goes back to the restaurant?"

"He won't." The memory of that last sad glance shook her. She stuffed it away, out of reach. Out of mind. "I made sure of it."

When the class ended a half-hour later, Melanie followed Abby into the back storage room to the corner where she kept a desk with a phone and an old desktop computer. On the wall behind the chair she'd hung the poster she'd purchased at the Belly Dance Divas show she and Melanie had attended the previous summer.

"You finally put it up," Melanie said, admiring the image. "It looks good. Not as good as it would if I were in the lineup, but good."

"When they add you to the lineup, I'll buy a hundred of these posters and wallpaper every room with them," Abby said. She booted up the computer, grabbed the stack of bills from the wire in-box on the desk, and settled in to pay as many as her bank account allowed.

"Guess I better get busy then. Auditions are coming up fast."

"So what are you doing in here? Get in there," Abby said and jerked her thumb toward the empty dance room.

"Fine. I'm going."

It had become their usual Saturday routine. After the morning class, Abby attended to studio business and cleaned up, while Melanie worked on her audition choreography.

"You're such a taskmaster," Melanie said, "but I guess that's why I even have a chance at the Divas."

"No way, you did it all yourself. You have more natural talent than any dancer I know. I'm amazed how far you've come in just two years."

"I think I just lucked out and got a really good teacher."

It was an especially sweet thing to say. Melanie had been her first serious student. They'd met in Almira's class, when Abby was just one of several class assistants. Melanie had asked Almira for private lessons, but the instructor declined, saying she was cutting back on her workload. She suggested Abby as an alternate.

It had surprised Abby, and given her a much-needed dose of confidence.

She and Melanie had formed a friendship during those private lessons that had grown quickly. Abby trusted Melanie more than anyone, and if Melanie hadn't helped her get the job at the newspaper, she would probably be standing in an unemployment line somewhere.

Melanie put her hand on Abby's shoulders. "It's going to be okay. You know that, right? You're meant to be here."

Abby fought a sudden spring of tears because at that moment, she really wasn't sure.

"I hope you're right."

CHAPTER FOURTEEN

WHEN DEREK STEPPED off the elevator at seven-fifteen Monday morning, the fifth floor was silent and empty. Most employees didn't arrive until eight or nine, which gave him some time to start investigating his options. He already had the call in to his lawyer and his stockbroker. He had just a few other calls to make and then he could get started on that other matter he wanted to investigate. The one that was making it impossible to sleep.

He caught a whiff of espresso. Fresh espresso. He followed it to the executive break room and nearly collided with someone backing out through the swinging door.

"Miss Anderson?" he asked. He wasn't sure because this woman looked like a librarian cliché, with her hair piled up high and tight and a pair of heavy black glasses on her nose. She didn't look at all like the mousy and skittish clerk he had met on Friday.

But he had startled her more than she startled him. She spun around, sending the steaming cappuccino splashing over the rim of her mug. She squealed, but the damage was done.

"I'm sorry, Mr. Collier! I didn't know anyone else was here. I wanted to settle in before you arrived."

So it was Miss Anderson. At least that mystery was solved.

Frantically she disappeared back through the door and emerged again without her mug and clutching a handful of paper napkins. She patted his sleeves where the coffee had rained on him.

He took the napkins and motioned her back.

"It's all right. I think I was spared most of it. The floor didn't fare so well."

She glanced down at the wet spot in the carpet between them and groaned. She disappeared through the door and returned with another wad of napkins. Dropping to her knees, she attempted to rub the coffee out of the carpet with the napkins. It only left a trail of white bits everywhere she touched.

"Don't worry about that, Miss Anderson," he said. "Call someone from maintenance."

She started to argue, but stopped. She rose and composed herself, though her glance remained cast down. "Of course, I'll call downstairs right away. Can I get you anything? A cappuccino? An espresso?"

"Yeah," he said, marveling at her turnaround and the astonishing change in her appearance. Was it the hair? The glasses? If he had seen her on the street he would not even guess she was the woman he had hired on Friday. He rubbed at his lip. "An espresso, if you don't mind," he said, distracted. "Three sugars."

"Very good, I'll bring it to your office," she said, turned on her heels, and slipped back into the break room.

A few minutes later he heard a tap at his door.

"Come in." He tucked away the manila folder he had been reading.

She stood at the open door looking perplexed.

"Won't you be working out of the publisher's office?"

"Since I'm the publisher now, doesn't that make any office I choose the publisher's office?"

Hot pink crept up her collar. "Of course it does, sir."

He should apologize. He knew that. It wasn't her fault he'd just found this blasted folder and a dozen others on his desk. Left by his father, no doubt. Just trying to be helpful, no doubt.

"I prefer to give my father a chance to collect his things." His father had been eager to hand over the publisher reins, but not so eager to leave the office. He told Derek he could use it any time, but really, when was he going to use the old man's office? It felt like wearing someone else's shoes. He didn't like it.

"Certainly," she said. "Mildred cleared her desk— I mean, her former desk—but I can move my things closer, if you prefer. There's a desk here I could use."

There were several actually. The last round of layoffs had not touched the fifth floor as severely as it had other parts of the company, but two directors and their support staff had been let go.

"Move if you like, it makes no difference to me. Just forward my calls here. My espresso?"

"Excuse me?"

He pointed to her hands.

She looked down at the cup in her grip. "Right." She hurried forward and set the espresso on the corner of his desk. Deposited three sugar packets and a spoon alongside, and hurried back to the door.

How odd she was. Confident and self-assured one moment. Timid as a wet kitten the next. It was difficult to know what to make of her.

He emptied each of the sugar packets into his cup and stirred. She was still standing in the doorway when he was finished. "Is there something else?"

"I hope you don't mind," she said, still watching the floor as she spoke. "But I took the liberty of filling in your calendar with the meetings Mildred said your father typically attends during the week. Let me know if you'd like any changes, and I'll be happy to make them."

Newspaper business. He'd nearly forgotten there was a routine he would be expected to uphold in addition to everything else.

"I'll have a look. Thank you."

There was another awkward pause when she didn't leave.

"Is there anything else, Miss Anderson?"

She hesitated, then blurted, "What do you want me to do?"

CHAPTER FIFTEEN

Thud!

Abby stared at the stack of manila folders that had just landed on her desk.

"I would appreciate it if you would compile this into a spreadsheet for me. I'd do it myself, but I have about three minutes to get to an editorial meeting and I need to stop by Finance. Any questions?" Derek's gaze was already on the elevator.

Yeah, about a hundred of them. Instead, she asked one. "What do you want in the spreadsheet?"

He shrugged. "I don't know. Tell me what you'd want to know if these companies were trying to buy something from you. And I need it as soon as possible. There's a board meeting coming up to discuss the bidders, and I want to know who we're dealing with." He walked away.

"No problem," she murmured to his back. "It's what I'm here for."

Is that what she was here for? She had no idea what an executive assistant was supposed to do.

The training she had received from Mildred on Friday afternoon had included how to answer the phone, where the files were kept, and where the steno pads were, because she assumed Derek, like his father, would prefer to dictate his correspondence. The poor woman had been horrified to discover Abby didn't know shorthand. The only useful thing the woman had taught her was how to operate the monstrous beverage machine in the executive break room.

Thank God she had, too, because the cappuccinos that came out of that thing could make working on the polar ice cap bearable. Abby lifted her mug, sipped, and tried to make sense of the folders fanned out in front of her. Darthshire Investments. Brandywine Corporation. Smith and Jergen Inc. At least a dozen more. All companies that wanted to buy the Collier Media Group.

Tell him what she'd want to know, huh? Okay. Start with the obvious. Annual earnings. Debt ratio. Public or private. Revenue history. Revenue outlook. Base of operations. Number of employees. How long in business. Corporate officers.

She opened a new spreadsheet on the computer and started labeling rows under a column titled "Darthshire." As she worked she made other notes. Where were the principals from? Where did they go to school? Did they have families? Anything she could dig up on the Internet.

Three hours later, she had compiled a hefty dossier on Darthshire and its board.

One down, twenty to go.

Melanie found her still at it at lunchtime.

"Hey, are you going to break for—"

She paused when Abby glanced up and then broke into barking laughter.

"Be quiet," Abby pleaded, glancing around the corner to see if the vice president's executive assistant had overheard. The woman had done little more than glare at Abby since she arrived. Sore she'd been passed over for the promotion, no doubt. Abby didn't want to give her any more reason to be unpleasant. Luckily, Gladys was nowhere to be seen and Derek's door had been shut since he returned from his morning meetings.

"But those glasses," Melanie whispered. "You look like you stepped out of a *Mad Men* episode."

"I thought they'd help." She squirmed in her seat.

Melanie pulled back and scrutinized her. "Actually, they do. I barely recognize you. The hair. The glasses. And those clothes. My God, Abby, where did you find that outfit? A plaid skirt? Honestly?"

"Okay. Maybe I overdid it."

"Ya think? But what do I know? I guess you have to do what you have to do."

"Did you just come up here to harass me?"

"No. I didn't see you in the cafeteria, so I came up to remind you to eat lunch."

Abby rolled her eyes. "Do you see all this? I have to get through it all."

Melanie tugged one of the folders on the desk so she could read the label.

Abby gathered them all up and dropped them in her drawer. "But you're right. I have to eat something.

I've been guzzling cappuccinos all morning. If I drink any more, I'll probably vomit."

"Cappuccinos?"

"Have you seen the cappuccino maker they have up here?"

Melanie shook her head.

"Oh, you have to see this." Abby pulled Melanie toward the break room. At the doorway, she gestured like Vanna White at the massive copper contraption.

"It's like a work of art. Man, this job has some perks," Melanie said, her eyes wide with wonder. "Maybe it was a mistake letting you have it. I should have taken it for myself." She nudged Abby with her elbow. "Just kidding. It's all yours. But if those babies come in a to-go cup . . ."

"Sure," Abby said. "I'm practically a barista now."

When they both had cappuccinos in hand, they headed toward the elevator. Abby caught Melanie craning for a look into Derek's office.

Abby tugged her friend to keep moving.

"You can't blame a girl for trying to get a glimpse. He is pretty hot."

"Hey!"

"Just kidding. C'mon."

"Maybe I should let him know I'm going downstairs. Just in case he needs something."

"Right," Melanie smirked. "Just in case."

She ignored Melanie and approached the door. Derek was on his phone, she could hear him through the door. She knocked softly. Nothing. She knocked again. Still nothing. She turned the knob and leaned in.

He was turned around in his chair, looking out over the eastern foothills. "I don't care, Frank. I'm not my father. You said you would have those bylaws to me today, so I want them today. Do you understand? I want to know if there's anything that can derail this sale, and you're not being paid to spend the day on the golf course. So get in here, and do your damn job."

Alarm bells went off in her head.

"Good," Derek continued, "I'll expect them by the end of the day." He spun around in his chair and slammed the receiver down as Abby was pulling the door closed.

"What the hell were you doing in here?" he hollered after her.

"I'm sorry," she said, returning. "I didn't know it was a bad time. I just wanted you to know I was taking my lunch."

She may as well have said she wanted to grow a second head.

"Rule number one around here: knock first." He gave her a look like she was dumber than dirt and picked up the phone again. He dismissed her with a flip of his wrist.

"What was that about?" Melanie whispered when Abby closed the door.

"He's busy" was all she could say, but inside she was reeling. How could that be the same man who had been so kind and tender? It didn't matter. In fact, it made it easier. All she had to do was keep her head down, do her job, and cash in when the time came.

CHAPTER SIXTEEN

DAMN. THE OLD man was already up, sitting at the end of the long granite island, sipping his coffee. His glance slid up from his morning paper at the sound of Derek's footsteps.

"Six a.m.? I'm beginning to think you're avoiding me."

"Just stopped by to pick up a few things," Derek said.

"Are you going somewhere?" He nudged his chin toward the garment bag folded over Derek's arm.

"I took a villa at the Bay Club. Closer to the office. More convenient."

"More convenient? I see." His father sipped his coffee.

Sure, it was a lie and his father knew it. But there was no point telling him he couldn't live under the same roof. They both knew how difficult it had been between them, even when Mother was around. She had been the bridge that could bring them together. But when she left, it took whatever was left of their relationship with it. Even on Derek's brief visits, he found no solace within these walls. No laughter or joy. Only cold furnishings, and a colder man who locked himself in his study to pore over account ledgers and God knows what else. The only love left in this house was a love of wealth and status, and Derek vowed to himself he would never follow that path. "Did you get up early just to check up on me?"

"No, actually. I thought you would want to know the board has moved up the vote on the sale."

A muscle in Derek's jaw twitched. "You said that wouldn't come for a few months."

His father snapped the paper and began reading again. "Things change, son. It's better this way. The quicker the better, all around. Have your secretary prepare the board room for Thursday afternoon."

All around? Hardly. It certainly wasn't better for him. It was a damn nuisance, in fact. "I'm sure you're right, Father. You're always right."

He wasn't going to linger. On the way into the office, he rang his lawyer. The call went to voice mail. "Listen, Frank, we need to move quickly. As in immediately."

Frank always promised he could work miracles. It was a good thing, because he needed one now.

He didn't realize he was speeding down Coast Highway until he neared the Sultan's Tent and pulled back on the accelerator. It wasn't exactly on the way to the paper, but it had become his habit these past few days. Not that he thought he would see her, not this time of day, but it was the only thing that stirred something besides anger and frustration inside him.

It helped, but when he stepped out of the elevator into the fifth-floor reception lobby, his mind was still churning. Adrenaline coursed through him. What he needed was an hour in the gym to work off the anger, but he didn't have time.

"Any calls?" he barked at Miss Anderson as he passed her.

She shook her head.

"Get Frank Jetter on the line, will you?" He paused a beat. "No, forget it. I'll do it myself."

He pulled out his desk chair and noticed a familiar stack of folders on his desk.

"What are these doing here?" he yelled at his assistant.

She appeared in the doorway. "Your files. Most of them, at least. I'm still working on a few. But I've finished the reports on those."

He flipped open the folder labeled Darston LLC. On top, she had placed a sheet that contained a carefully organized summary of the business.

"And this is the comparative spreadsheet you requested." She stepped forward and handed him a thin, brass-bradded report.

"Fine," he said. "This should be helpful." He knew he should say more. It was staggeringly impressive. How had she found the time? "Did you include financial data?"

"Yes. And I'll have the remaining reports to you by tomorrow morning, along with an updated comparative spreadsheet."

"That's fine," he said, already distracted by the spreadsheet.

"Do you need anything else?"

She was still staring at the ground, but there was something different about her. A new confidence. She obviously knew what she was doing. He closed the folder. "Have you had any luck getting the company bylaws from our attorney?"

"This came for you this morning." She pointed to a fat manila envelope on his desk.

He ripped it open. Bylaws. Perfect. He could spend the morning going through it.

His line rang.

"I'll get it," she said.

He watched her leave. And the way her pencil skirt hugged her hips. So there was a figure in there. Quite a nice one, by the looks of it. Why'd she hide it?

She stuck her head in the doorway. "It's your lawyer."

"I need to take that. Would you close the door?"

When she did as he asked, he scooped up the phone receiver. "Tell me you have good news."

"Sorry," Frank said. "It's not that easy. Can you get up here this morning?"

When he didn't answer right away, Frank added, "It's important."

"Fine."

When Derek emerged from his office, Miss Anderson was nowhere to be found. He checked the break room. The corridor. So frustrating. That was the problem with people. Just when you think you can count on them, they let you down. They always let you down. He was storming his way to the elevator to ask the vice president's assistant if she had seen Abby when he found her, standing in the fifth-floor lobby in front of a collection of framed historic front pages from the *Herald*'s archives. "Man Walks on the Moon," emblazoned on one. "Nixon Resigns," "Berlin Wall Comes Down," and others.

She seemed to be examining the old black-and-white photos that also hung there. The one of the single-story building the newspaper had occupied in the 1950s when his grandfather had bought it, and another from the 1970s, just after construction was completed on the current building. He held back, watching her observe the images. How many times over the years had he lingered there? Far too many to count. Just staring at those images, feeling the connection to his grandfather and that old man's struggle to build this newspaper from a penny circular into a Pulitzer-winning news enterprise.

That old man had so much drive, so much passion for what he did. He had it till the day he died. The way his eyes had sparked when he spoke about the paper and the importance of getting news to the public. It had sparked the same fire in Derek. Was he seeing it in Abby's eyes, as well?

Those dark, knowing eyes hiding behind those black-rimmed glasses. There was definitely something different about her today. He stepped forward. "Miss Anderson, I need to speak to you."

"Of course," she said, startled but recovering quickly. "I was just waiting for Gladys to print the VP's weekly report."

"It's nearly finished," the silver-haired woman snapped from behind her desk. "I'll deliver it when it's done."

Back in his office, he handed her the bylaws. "Can you go through these? It should be pretty standard, but I'd like to know if there's anything that could hold up the sale."

She flipped through the thick stack. "Sure." She tilted her head and glanced up. "I guess I didn't realize how hard this must be for you."

He grabbed his jacket from the coat rack. "Excuse me?"

"I'm sorry," she mumbled and buried her gaze in the stack of paper. "I was just looking at those pictures and it hit me. This must be really hard for you. So much pressure to fill your father's shoes. Your grandfather's shoes."

He didn't know what to say. It was like she had ripped a hole right through him. "I guess it is."

"It's quite a legacy."

"It would have been."

"Does it bother you?"

"Of course it does." He closed his briefcase and stood over it, paralyzed. "All my life, I've been told I would run this place one day. I used to hate the idea of it. I didn't want that decision to be made for me. But now that I won't have it—" He couldn't finish the thought.

The way the light caught her eye. It was . . . he couldn't put his finger on it. He was lucky to have her in his corner. She was smart, savvy, compassionate. And what she lacked in looks, she made up for in so many other ways. If things were different, he might—

No. His plans were already in the works. In a day or two he would know something useful.

But, damn, he wasn't used to being the pursuer.

He was used to fending off advances, not making them. He was used to deflecting unwanted attention. There was always someone angling for a favor. Someone who wanted to be seen on the Collier heir's arm. In six years, he hadn't found a single woman who didn't have ulterior motives.

Maybe that's what made Zenina so different. She had seen his car. Seen the hotel. Even if she didn't know his name, she was smart enough to know what he was worth.

And she hadn't cared. It was just about the best thing about her. Well, next to that tattoo that wrapped her hips and belly like the sexiest damn gift he'd ever seen.

He felt a twitch beneath his belt. He had to stop or he wasn't going to get any work done today. And the way it was shaping up, he had more to do now than ever.

"I gotta go," he said. "Reschedule my appointments. I'll be back after lunch."

CHAPTER SEVENTEEN

ABBY COULDN'T PUT her finger on it, but something was definitely up with Derek today.

Not only had he let her skate by with unfinished work, but he was almost civil. Or was that her imagination?

It didn't matter. At least when she'd handed over the incomplete spreadsheet and told him she'd have the rest of the reports to him the next day, he hadn't asked for those remaining files, because they were still in her apartment, sitting right where she'd left them beside her home computer, along with a copy of the bylaws. Her plan to be a superstar assistant would have worked out so much better if she hadn't slept through her alarm. In her rush to get herself ready and out the door, she'd left half the project behind. Thankfully, she had e-mailed herself what she had finished, so she had something to give him.

He had been surprisingly fine with the incomplete package, and then when he'd found her waiting by Gladys's desk, he'd been downright pleasant.

Just like that first night.

The idea caught her in a way she didn't expect. She had tried to forget that night. Of course she hadn't, but she pushed it from her thoughts every time it surfaced. She told herself how pointless it was, how dangerous.

The logical side of her listened.

But there was another side that still wanted him. Maybe now more than ever. He had been so wonderful that first night. Gorgeous and perfect. On his best behavior, the way new lovers always are.

These last few days she had seen the real man. The one who was as passionate about his work and his family as he was in the bedroom. He wouldn't be so angry or feel so betrayed if he wasn't.

And she had to give him credit. If her family betrayed her the way his had betrayed him, she wouldn't be taking it nearly so well. She certainly wouldn't help them twist the knife once they'd stabbed her in the back.

She could see his pain. He didn't want this sale. That was obvious now. He was not as impenetrable as he pretended to be. She glimpsed that soft, tender lover again, in moments, and it nearly undid her.

She thought of her father, and the life ripped away from him. And herself, having her only living parent taken from her. She knew about pain and loss. She knew the way it twisted up your insides.

Maybe if she told Derek she understood. Maybe if she wrapped herself around him as she had that night.

It was stupid to even consider. She couldn't declare herself now. He'd never forgive her.

Would he? Could she make him understand why she had lied?

At her desk, she scribbled a message on a sticky note. "Back in 10. Running downstairs."

But she didn't go downstairs. She needed to make a call and it had to be private. She found her car in the parking structure, crawled into the driver's seat, and shut the door. On her phone, she dialed Melanie.

Her friend picked up on the third ring. "Hey, what's up?"

"You need to talk me out of doing something really stupid."

"Okay," Melanie said. "What would that be exactly?"

"I want to tell him the truth."

CHAPTER EIGHTEEN

BY THE TIME ABBY returned to the executive floor fifteen minutes later, she was feeling better. Melanie had done exactly as Abby had hoped: Made her see how suicidal it would be to come clean with Derek. At least right now. Give it some time, Melanie advised. If something developed down the road, tell him then. Just wait until the studio was no longer on the line.

She didn't tell Melanie that road would be a short one, since a sale was imminent. It was difficult enough keeping that secret from Melanie.

But her friend would understand. It was the practical thing to do.

When Abby returned to her desk, Derek's office door was nearly closed and she heard voices. He was back already? Had he been looking for her?

She went to the door to let him know she was back, but his voice reached her before she reached the door.

"She works at the Sultan's Tent?"

Abby froze. It was a second voice she didn't recognize.

"Yes," Derek answered. "Thursday and Friday nights. I'm sure you'll find her there."

"That will probably be enough to get started."

"Will it, or won't it? I don't want a probably."

"If it isn't, I'll make some calls. I can find what I need."

"Good."

"So, is this a story assignment? My editor wasn't clear on the details."

"It's not for the newspaper."

Was this for real? Abby tried to breathe, tried not to pass out.

"Then, how should I note it on my expense report?"

"No expense report," Derek shot back. "No time cards, either. Just let me know the hours and what you spend. I'll pay you."

"Directly?"

The young man was obviously struggling to understand. Abby didn't blame him. She wasn't doing any better.

"I guess I'm just not sure why you asked me to do this," he continued. "Why do you need a reporter?"

"Because you know how to dig up information. You know how to get a story. I want this woman's story. Write up everything you find and give it to me. Directly."

"Seems like a lot of trouble—"

"Your editor told me you're the best at what you do. That's why you're here. But if you prefer I ask someone else, I'm sure I can find someone interested in making an extra grand."

"A thousand dollars?" The words all but sputtered out of the guy's mouth. "No, I mean, I want the job, I was just—"

"You know the place. You know what I want. Tell me you can have your report to me first thing Monday morning and we're finished."

"I will have my report to you first thing Monday morning, Mr. Collier."

The sound of movement startled Abby out of her paralysis. She slid quickly into her desk chair. Blood thrummed in her ears. Fear hammered on her chest.

She watched the reporter exit the office and walk by her desk. Tall. Thin. Bookish. Her unwitting executioner.

He eyed her on his way to the elevator. "Good afternoon."

"Good afternoon," she replied and dropped her glance.

Was that the world crumbling beneath her feet?

CHAPTER NINETEEN

ABBY STARED AT the bylaws on her desk, but she hadn't been able to read a complete sentence for well over an hour. She could only see that reporter's face. And imagine what Derek's face would look like, once he learned the truth.

There was no way around that now. Damn, she should have just been honest from the beginning.

"What are you still doing here, Miss Anderson?"

She hadn't heard Derek's door open. She hadn't heard him walk up behind her. Oh, God. How was she going to face him?

"I was just . . . the bylaws. I was reading through them like you asked." Her tongue felt like chalk.

"You don't have to finish that tonight. Go home. Pick it up tomorrow."

He was so calm. So pleasant. It made what she had to do even more difficult.

"Actually, can I speak with you?"

He checked his smartphone. "Can it wait? I'm running late."

If only it could.

"It'll only take a minute."

Just long enough for him to say "You're fired," most likely.

His lips pinched. "All right."

"Can we do it in your office?"

Had she really just said that? She wanted to hide her face in her hands, but there wasn't time to be embarrassed. She couldn't see his face. Maybe he hadn't registered the ill-chosen words.

And maybe she was making a mountain out of a molehill. Maybe he would even think this whole thing was funny.

And maybe monkeys would fly out of her ears.

She followed him into his office. He leaned against his desk and crossed his arms.

"Okay, what's so urgent?" he said.

Her fingers rolled into fists at her sides, clutching at nothing as this roller coaster car pulled out of the depot.

"I heard you speaking with the reporter."

He straightened and scowled. "That's a private matter. It doesn't concern you."

"But it does." She nearly choked on the words. Seeing him look at her in that cold, brutal way. There had been such warmth in his eyes that first night. Such passion and fire. She remembered stroking the edge of that smooth jaw, the hard lines of his face. She opened her mouth to speak. Nothing came out. She turned away.

As long as she didn't look at him, she could breathe. She could think. She could remember what she had to say. She pulled a stray tendril behind her ear. Slid the glasses to the top of her head like a head band and turned back to him. "I'm Zenina."

It wasn't anger she saw on his face. It was . . . amusement. A smile turned his cheek. He shook his head. "Miss Anderson, I don't know what kind of game you're playing. But this isn't the way to go about it."

He didn't believe her. She hadn't expected that. "But I am."

He was still shaking his head, chuckling.

It was maddening. Irritating. "Why would I lie about that?"

"Why do women lie about anything?" he said. "It beats me. But it is a lie. I don't know how you found out about Zenina. But you are not her. Believe me. She's—" He paused. He stared at the ground. "She's different, Miss Anderson."

Her fear metabolized into something different. Something beyond irritation. "Different? Really? You might not recognize me, but I bet you'll recognize this." She worked the buttons on her black blouse and threw it open, not caring that it exposed the simple, white bra beneath. Only certain that he would not doubt her when he saw the tattoo.

The smirk dropped from his face. He inched toward her. His eyes locked on her belly. When he was close enough, he reached out. Fingertips trailed the lines that looped around her waist and plunged beneath the waistband of her skirt.

He stared in silence for a moment before his gaze lifted to hers.

She could see he believed her. Relief mingled with ecstasy. Would he embrace her? Kiss her? She ached to feel him against her, and in that moment she knew. She wanted him—had never stopped wanting him. Not for one night, but until the world ended. She couldn't deny it anymore. She loved him.

CHAPTER TWENTY

"ZENINA?" DEREK SAID the name, but he couldn't convince himself it was real. Nothing felt real. Was the room tilting? Was he still breathing? He didn't know. He could only see her, staring up at him. What was that shine in her eyes? Pride? Triumph? For what? He didn't understand.

From the pit of his stomach, a raw, gnawing feeling punched back at the question until there was no thought but this: She had lied to him. When had it started? How deep did it run? It didn't matter. All that mattered was the wrenching in his gut. The feeling of being used. That all-too-familiar anguish. She didn't want him. She had never wanted him. She only wanted his position. His power. She wanted what she could take from him. She was just like the others.

His fingers burned where they touched her skin and he snatched them back.

Self-consciously she tugged the edges of her shirt closed.

"Get out," he whispered.

The way her dark eyes flashed, he could see she hadn't expected it. Her smile faded. The victory in her eyes vanished. She was the one suffering now.

It gave him only a little satisfaction, but it was enough.

"But, Derek, everything was—"

He raised his hand to stop her. It didn't matter what she said now. He knew the truth. "Just leave."

She stood, frozen. Her expression chiseled with misery and regret.

Fine, if she wouldn't leave, he would. Without another word, without a glance, he brushed past her and was out the door.

CHAPTER TWENTY-ONE

THE FIRST TIME Abby heard the knock on her front door, she thought it was the television. She was on the sofa, passing in and out of sleep between reruns of *Smallville*, *Angel*, and *Charmed*.

The second time the thumps rattled the walls.

She rolled over and pulled her blanket over her head. Go away.

"Abby, are you in there?"

It was Melanie. Ugh. What did she want? Abby peeked over her shoulder at the DVD player's digital clock. Nine thirty-eight. Already? The gray light filtering through the blinds made her think it was earlier. Sunny Southern California, yeah, right. Marine layers and May Gray was more like it.

Nine thirty-eight. She should be at her desk. She'd probably be on her second, maybe third cappuccino, if she hadn't screwed things up.

She forced herself up and went to the door, the blanket trailing behind her.

Melanie looked her up and down. "What the hell happened to you?"

Abby stepped aside to let her friend in.

"What are you doing here?" she said.

"I could ask you the same question." Melanie gaped at the mess in the living room. The blankets and pillows. The empty bowls and bent soda cans. The ice cream carton and melted chocolate puddle on the coffee table. "Looks like a junk food tornado came through here."

"I wasn't expecting company." She took a half-hearted pass around the room, picking up.

"I went up to the fifth floor to see you and ran into Tall, Dark, and Moody. He said—and not exactly kindly, I might add—that you don't work for him anymore. What the hell happened? And why have you been ignoring my texts?"

"What texts?" Abby deposited the dirty dishes in the sink and grabbed her purse from the shoulder of a chair. She pulled out her smartphone. Eight missed messages. All from Melanie. None from Derek. But then, did she really expect to hear from him? He'd made it pretty clear he never wanted to see her again. After he told her to leave and walked out, she'd grabbed her purse and left, too.

The rest of the day—and night—was a wet, blubbering blur. She'd cried about losing Derek, and then her job, and soon the studio. And then that pain had tangled up with the familiar, year-old heartache. All the names her ex had called her, all those things he'd said. Maybe they were truer than she wanted to admit. Maybe she was damaged goods. It was her own selfishness that had driven Derek away. Her deception. If she'd been honest, if she'd been worthy. But she wasn't. That was the cruel, awful truth and she might as well face it.

She thought there could be no tears left, but fresh ones streamed down her face.

"Hey, hey, hey." Melanie came up and put a comforting arm around her shoulder. "Seriously, what happened?"

"Everything," Abby managed to say between sobs. "I ruined everything. With Derek. With the studio. And it's all my own fault."

"Okay, this is what we're going to do," Melanie said in a soothing tone that belied the directive. "I'm going to make us some tea. And you're going to tell me everything."

At the end of it, Abby took a calm, restorative breath. She didn't feel good, but she felt better.

"So let's see if I have this right," Melanie said. "You've pretty much lost your only chance to save the studio, and you realize you love this guy, but now he doesn't want anything to do with you."

Abby nodded. That almost good feeling was slipping away. "Yep," she said. "In a nutshell."

Melanie paced as she pondered the problem. She stopped at the dinette table, and stared at Abby's laptop and the file folders stacked beside it. "What's this?"

"Work." Sometime around midnight, she'd realized that while she had lost her chance to save the studio, it was the betrayal in Derek's eyes that hurt the deepest. She wanted to do something—anything—to make it up to him. The files she'd forgotten at home the day before were still sitting on her table, staring at her. That's when she'd decided to finish what she had started. She'd completed all but the last bidder profile and finished reading the bylaws, noting anything that might disrupt a sale. It wasn't going to make up for what she'd done, but it was all she had. And for a few hours, it had kept her mind off of everything else.

That final mysterious bidder vexed her, though. There wasn't even a file for it. Just one typed sheet she'd found stuck in a paper clip to another bidder's folder. It contained the company name (DRC Enterprises), city of business (Newport Beach), and a vague statement of intent. Internet searches brought up nothing. A DBA search didn't bring up anything, either.

"Why are you still working on this? He fired you."

"I know."

"You're crazy, you know that?"

Abby shrugged.

"So here's what I don't get," Melanie said. "If you knew that reporter was going to rat you out, you could've done something. You could've quit the restaurant. You could've changed your dance name. Any number of things."

"I know." All those possibilities had entered her mind, too. But she'd rejected them. "He deserves to know the truth. I wanted him to know."

"Even though it ruined everything?"

Abby nodded. "I know. It's stupid, but I love him."

It was strange to hear the word aloud. Somehow it made it even more real. She loved him. She loved the sweet and tender lover he had been. She even loved the tyrant he could be at work. She knew he only acted the way he did because he was so passionate about the paper and it pained him to oversee its sale. Truthfully, she didn't want him chasing a phantom Zenina. She wanted him to know that the woman he wanted was her.

"So what about the studio?"

"What about it? I think it's obvious I'm not cut out for it. It's barely been a year, and I've already lost it."

"No, you haven't."

"I appreciate your vote of confidence, but I know I have. You've seen the notices. I have a month to catch up on rent before I'm out. And that's money I don't have."

"But maybe you will after this weekend."

"What are you talking about?"

"I know you said you didn't have time to check around about the rules on holding benefits, but it just so happens that I do. Or did. Because I did some research and you'll be happy to know there's nothing stopping you from holding one."

"You did that for me?" Tears flooded her eyes again. She pulled Melanie into a hug. "That's probably the nicest thing anyone has ever done for me and I love you for it, but there's no way I can pull together a show in a week. I don't think I could do it in a month."

Melanie pulled back.

"As it happens, I think you can. I have it on excellent authority that at least two of the Belly Dance Divas will be in town and are more than happy to perform. It's for a good cause, and it's great publicity for them. And not only that, I've already given the information to the entertainment editor at the paper and she's going to get it into Friday's events calendar.

I even stopped in and talked to the Saturday night dancer at the Sultan's Tent, and she said she'd be happy to cover your night. I mean, if you're still opposed to my bellygram idea."

Abby could hardly believe it.

"The Belly Dance Divas are going to perform at the Shimmy Shop? Are you kidding me? How could I turn that down?"

"I was hoping you'd say that. Now, listen. I know we won't be able to raise all that you need, but I think we can raise a thousand or two. And maybe it'll be enough to buy you more time."

Abby shook her head. It was a lot to take in. "How long have you been working on this?"

"A few days."

"But how'd you keep it secret?"

"I didn't. Not really. You've just been preoccupied."

"I guess I have. Well, as soon as I finish up this work for Derek, I'm going to dedicate one hundred percent of my time to promoting this event."

Melanie cocked her head. "You're still going to finish? That's insane. He fired you. What part of that don't you understand? How about I just take these files back with me and you focus on the studio." She went to the table and grabbed up the folders.

Abby stopped Melanie's hand. "I want to finish. I need to."

They stared at one another, each holding her ground. Melanie was the first to pull back.

"Okay, fine. Let's finish it, now, together. Then I'm taking these files back with me, and you're done." She picked up the mystery sheet and started reading it. "So what are we doing? What's DRC Enterprises?"

"It's one of the bidders for the newspaper."

Melanie dropped the sheet. "It's what?"

"Yeah," Abby said, wincing. "The newspaper is for sale. All of Collier Media Group is for sale. That's what I've been doing. Researching prospective buyers. That's why Derek was brought in, and that's why he's been such a tyrant. He doesn't want to do it. I know he doesn't."

"You knew about this going in?"

"He told me during the interview. They promised me a great severance package . . . Well, it doesn't matter anymore. But the only people who would be out of jobs would be him and me, and probably some of the other top-floor executives. No one else, especially not you. I swear. I made him promise that." She could see Melanie was thinking exactly what she would be thinking.

"He said any new buyer would need to hire staff, not let any go," she hurried to add. "The cuts last year were too deep, he said. You are not going to lose your job. I would have told you if your job was in trouble."

"I guess I should have seen it coming. But geez, Abby, why are you doing all this for a company that was going to let you go anyway?"

"I'm not doing it for the company. I'm doing it for Derek. I know he hates me, but he needs this. It's bad enough that he's losing his newspaper. If he can make sure it goes to a good buyer, maybe it will be less painful."

"You really have it bad for that guy, don't you? So that's what all this is, information on the bidders?" Melanie gravitated to the piles of paperwork again and started flipping through files.

"Some of them. I've been putting together corporate profiles on each, but this one I can't find any details about at all." She handed the mystery bid sheet back to Melanie. "Have you ever heard of DRC Enterprises?"

"Doesn't ring a bell." She gazed at it a while longer. "Says they're based in Newport Beach. Did you run a DBA search in the county's database?"

"Yeah. Nothing."

"Check with the state board of equalization?"

"Yeah. Same thing."

"Maybe it's an acronym that stands for something else. Delivery. Direct. Driven."

"Derek."

Melanie glanced up. "What?"

Was it that simple? Derek Rutherford Collier Enterprises. Was that why the sheet looked so out of place? As though it had slipped in, unnoticed? Maybe she was never supposed to see it. Maybe he wasn't trying to find a new buyer at all.

Suddenly, the phone calls to his attorney and all those closed-door conversations began to make sense. He wasn't looking for a buyer, he wanted to be the buyer. She shook her head. It was crazy. It was quixotic.

It was wonderful.

But could one Collier really buy out the rest of the family?

Something she'd seen in the bylaws came back to her. Something that hadn't seemed important . . . until now.

"Why are you smiling?" Melanie looked perplexed.

"I have to talk to Derek. If he's doing what I think he's doing, I have to tell him what I found. I think I know how he can save his company."

CHAPTER TWENTY-TWO

THE FIRST TIME Abby called Derek's number, she hung up when it went to voice mail. The second time, she left a message.

"Derek, I know you don't want to hear from me, but I have to talk to you. It's important."

She knew the moment she hung up that he wouldn't call back. She needed to be specific. She needed to tell him why he had to call. She tried again.

"Derek," she said when she was funneled into the voice mail system again. "I think I know what you're trying to do and there's something in the bylaws that can help you. I'm going to send you an e-mail with all the information. Please open it."

Sure, she sounded desperate. Maybe even insane. But she was. She couldn't untell the lie she had told him, or undo the damage she had caused, but she could do this. He would never forgive her, but in some small way, maybe she could at least make things better.

Still, it was risky. She knew he didn't check e-mails. He'd wait for a new assistant to do it, if he even got one. Which could take days, and come much too late to do any good.

For two hours, she sat on the sofa, staring at the television. Telling herself that she had done what she could. That it was out of her hands.

If only she hadn't sent the files back with Melanie. If she had those, she could use them as an excuse to return to the office. She could find a way to cross paths with him, and tell him what he needed to know.

Maybe Melanie would do it. She grabbed the phone and dialed her friend.

"Absolutely not," Melanie said when she heard Abby's plan. "I'm not going back up there. You wouldn't believe the look he gave me when I said I was returning them for you. I mean, seriously, I was doing him a favor and you'd think I'd just stolen his puppy. Why can't you do it yourself?"

"I had to surrender my employee badge. I can't get past reception."

"It's probably just as well. You should just forget about that guy. He's bad news. He's got the vice president's secretary helping him put together some urgent board meeting, and by noon that poor woman looked like she'd run a marathon. I'll bet money she calls in sick for the rest of the week just to avoid him."

An urgent board meeting. That had to be about the sale. Was it happening already?

"Please, Melanie," she pleaded. "I wouldn't ask if it wasn't important."

Melanie sighed. She was thinking it over.

"I would if I thought it would do any good, but it won't, Abby," she said finally. "I don't want to be involved, and honestly I don't think you should be, either. If he won't take your call, then send him a telegram or something. But I think you should drop it. You have the studio to worry about. Listen, I'll come by after work. I have some ideas about the benefit I want to run by you."

She hung up and Abby sat, stunned.

She'd run out of options.

And maybe Melanie was right. She needed to focus on the benefit. It was just two days away. Some of her advanced students had already left messages asking if they could perform and what they should wear.

Despite herself, she was getting excited. Even if they didn't make enough to save the place, it would at least be one hell of a farewell party.

But the problem with Derek still gnawed at her. And watching television wasn't helping. She had to focus on the benefit. Maybe picking out a costume for the event was a good place to start. She went to the closet where she kept her performance clothes, and sifted through the collection of harem pants and choli tops, veils and scarves and skirts. She pulled out a pair of magenta harem pants, considered them, then tossed them aside. A black pair she put aside, too. Too drab. Ah, the copper pair. Her favorite. Now those were worthy of a farewell performance.

She dropped her pajama bottoms and stepped into the silky copper pants, then searched for a choli. She decided on a silver-threaded black one and tied it on. She pulled on her brass-coin bra, and admired herself in a full-length mirror.

That Zenina feeling returned. The tough, fear nothing, ready for anything feeling. If only she'd had it when she'd declared herself to Derek. It might have made a difference. She wouldn't have let him walk out on her. She certainly wouldn't have done it without putting up a fight.

But did it matter? It was too late to do anything about it now.

Unless . . .

She dismissed the idea the instant it formed. It was too ridiculous. Too outrageous. It probably wouldn't even work.

But what if it did?

It wouldn't fix everything. It might not fix anything. But it just might get her through the door.

CHAPTER TWENTY-THREE

THE GUARD STARED at Abby as she approached the *Herald*'s main entrance. Would he recognize her? Would he stop her? She kept her eyes on the ground, and a portable speaker and the file clutched to her chest.

He said nothing as she pulled the door open. A good sign.

The real test was coming next. Jeanine, the lobby receptionist, a woman she'd seen every workday for the past four months. At the back, advertising and circulation representatives served customers, but the lobby waiting chairs were empty. Jeanine's attention remained on her computer.

"Birthday bellygram for Mr. Collier," Abby said when she reached the counter.

Jeanine looked up, her surprise quickly softened with a smile. "How wonderful! For our new Mr. Collier? I had no idea it was his birthday. Could you wait just a moment?" She dialed her phone and turned away from Abby.

Abby tried to listen to the woman's whispers into the receiver. Her stomach lurched. Her courage melted. What was she thinking coming here in costume? She'd hidden her face beneath layers of makeup and disguised her hair with more straps, feathers, and yarn than she'd ever used in her life. Not to mention the pounds of Middle Eastern pendants she'd added to her headdress. But was it enough? She was going to see people who had seen her every day. Someone was going to recognize her.

She was eyeing the door, mulling a quick escape when Jeanine put down the receiver.

"Here you go, honey," she said and handed a visitor badge over the counter.

Abby searched the woman's face for a glimmer of recognition. For the shock. The disapproval.

Jeanine only tapped the clipboard, as she did dozens of times a day for complete strangers. "If you could clip the badge somewhere and just sign in here."

A twenty-pound weight disappeared from Abby's shoulders. Quickly she scribbled, "Zenina, belly dancer."

"Through that door and take the elevator to the fifth floor. A woman named Gladys will be there to help you set up."

The relief of getting past Jeanine gave way to a fresh fear: facing the vice president's assistant. That woman had resented her from the moment she moved upstairs. Still, she took the badge, pinned it to her halter, and pushed through the door.

The looks were starting. She caught them in her peripheral vision. The long, curious glances. The rude, outright stares. She kept her eyes locked on the ground till she reached the elevator.

"Going up?"

She glanced up. It was only a guy in khakis she didn't recognize. She nodded, stepped into the car and pressed the fifth-floor button.

"Executive level, huh?" the guy said when he saw the light. "Those guys get all the perks."

She nodded again, but avoided eye contact. He might have been trying to make conversation, or it could have been something else. She didn't want to find out. She was just glad that when the car came to a stop on the third floor, he got off and no one else stepped on. "Good luck," he said as the door closed.

Yep. She was going to need it.

When the elevator stopped on the fifth floor, her chest was throbbing with fear. The doors slid open, and Gladys was there, peering down her nose. It didn't matter that Abby had a half-dozen scarves and belts draped around her hips, or her most modest choli. She was naked in front of this woman. Stripped to the bone. No pride. No dignity. Nothing. This was definitely a mistake. Whatever respect they might have had for Abby Anderson, the professional, would be history when they discovered her secret.

Abby stepped backwards, ready to flee.

"Are you Zenina?" Gladys stepped forward and held out her hand to shake.

No suspicion. No discernible disapproval.

Slowly, Abby straightened. "Yes, I'm Zenina." Saying it helped. I am Zenina. I *am* Zenina. Strong, bold, fearless.

"I can help you with that." Gladys reached for the speaker and the file. Abby tightened her hold. "No, thank you. I can manage." She glanced around and for the first time registered all the people sitting in the glass-walled conference room. Two dozen or more, men and women and all dressed in suits. It was the board meeting. Already in progress. This was not how she had envisioned it at all. She hadn't intended to face anyone, but possibly Derek. Just slip into his office and give him the folder.

"If you're looking for the young Mr. Collier, he's in a meeting," Gladys said. "You may have a seat while you wait."

She couldn't wait. What if it was already too late?

Abby ignored Gladys's invitation. She walked toward the conference room and spied Derek, sitting beside his father, at the head of the table. She found the door, and headed for it.

"Excuse me," Gladys said, rushing up to her. "You can't go in there. Please have a seat."

Abby heard the anxiety in the woman's voice, but it hardly registered. It was impossible to register anything but the rattling in her brain. The fear. The worry. The shame.

You have to do this. You must do this.

She gripped the folder to her chest. "I'm sorry. It has to be now."

By the time she opened the glass door, every pair of eyes around the table were fixed on her. She looked at Derek, who was staring with something between horror and rage.

Gladys burst in. "I'm so sorry for the interruption," she said. "I tried to have her wait, but she—"

"Thank you, Gladys," Derek said. He was on his feet and moving quickly. "I can take care of it from here."

Abby was too stunned to do anything but stand, frozen.

"In my office. Now, Miss Anderson," he growled.

Instantly murmurs circled the room.

Shame washed over her.

He grabbed her elbow and guided her—not quite roughly—toward the door.

"I don't know what you think you're trying to do here, Miss Anderson," he barked when they were in the corridor but still within earshot of the conference room. "If you think this is some kind of game or revenge, or if you're just trying to embarrass me, you can just quit right now."

She couldn't feel her feet. She couldn't feel anything—only the waves of condemnation surrounding her. This was everything she feared. She was naked and ashamed and alone.

"You wouldn't see me," she whispered, her eyes cast down. "I had to tell you—"

"We have nothing to say to each other, Miss Anderson," he said. "Nothing. I want you to leave."

There was no arguing with him. Not with any of them. Still, she had to do what she came here to do. She thrust the folder at him. "Just read this. It's all in here. Please just read it."

But he wasn't looking at her. No one was anymore. They were looking behind her. She turned.

Two security guards were there. She recognized one of them from the front door, and her heart plummeted.

The last spark of hope fizzled.

She could read the change in the expressions around her. No longer confusion or amusement. Just pity. Except for Derek. His read anger—straight and simple.

She turned and accepted the long, agonizing escort back to the main entrance—completely and utterly humiliated.

CHAPTER TWENTY-FOUR

MELANIE SCRATCHED HER head. "So, you sent yourself as a bellygram?"

"I wasn't really a bellygram," Abby insisted. "I just needed to get up to the fifth floor. To give him that folder. To tell him there's a chance he can save the paper."

"But you were dressed as a belly dancer, and you told Jeanine you were a belly dancer. So, how's that different from a bellygram?"

"Okay, fine, I was a bellygram."

"Just so we're clear. After all that griping about bellygrams degrading the art form, and blah, blah, blah."

"You could be a little more supportive, you know."

"Are you kidding? You didn't even call me. I missed the whole Zenina spectacle."

Abby wadded up an old class schedule from her studio desk and threw it at Melanie's head. "I wasn't a spectacle. Okay, maybe. A little. But only after I got to the fifth floor. That was pretty awful."

Melanie's laughter subsided. "Come on. How bad could it have been? A belly dancer in a room mostly full of men. It's not like it was a hostile crowd."

"You didn't see the way Derek looked at me. That was hostile. I'm such an idiot."

"Well, at least you got the information to him, right? So mission accomplished."

Tears welled in Abby's eyes. She fought them back and shook her head.

"You didn't give him the folder?"

"I don't know what happened to it. One minute I had it and the next the guards were showing me out and it was gone. It must have dropped somewhere, but there was no way they were going to let me go back and look for it."

"They called the security guards on you? Wow."

"Yeah, I'll never be able to show my face in that place again." Abby sank her head into her palms.

"Fine, so your grand plan backfired. It happens." Melanie was trying hard to be chipper. "I told you he was bad news. You should just forget all that and focus on what's important, like the benefit. Maybe something like which veils we should drape across the wall to make the stage. The purple or the red?" She held up two gauzy wads of chiffon.

Abby reached for a tissue and blew her nose. With another she dried her eyes. "I appreciate all the work you've done, and you've done a lot. You should know, though, that it's probably not going to be enough. I've used up everything. I've pushed back every bill I can. If I'm lucky, I can make it another month, maybe two."

"Don't be so glum. I have a good feeling about it. Word has really been spreading. I think you're going to be surprised by the turnout."

"You're right." She forced a brave face for Melanie. And if nothing else, it was going to be a great party.

CHAPTER TWENTY-FIVE

ABBY HAD SQUEEZED her way through the packed hallway and finally reached the storage room where the dancers were dressing when Melanie grabbed her arm.

"We should get started," her friend said, trying to be heard over the Middle Eastern music coming from the dance room. "Are you still planning to do an intro?"

It was a valid question because so far nothing was going according to plan. For two hours, people had been piling into the studio. The three dozen foldout chairs they had set up for audience seating had been filled long ago and now bodies pressed against walls, sprawled on the floor, and crowded into the hallway. The dressing room was no better. The two dancers from Belly Dance Divas had arrived on schedule, but they had coaxed the five other principal dancers to join them. It was a welcome surprise, but required a quick shuffling of the schedule and prep space to accommodate them.

Abby would have panicked if she hadn't already been in costume and makeup when she arrived to set up.

"Yeah, I still want to do it," she said. "Did you see the donation box? I've emptied it twice to make room for all the envelopes, and it's nearly full again. I don't know what you did to get so many people here, but wow. You must be some kind of PR genius."

Melanie cocked her head. "I thought it was you. I told some friends and asked them to post it online, and the entertainment editor put it into the paper's calendar, but that was it. I don't know half of these people and I have no idea where they came from. It's crazy."

Crazy only scratched the surface.

"How about letting me check on the dancers?" Melanie said. "You should go out there. The crowd's getting restless."

Abby could hear them. She made her way to the stage and took the microphone. The guy running the sound turned down the music, and the voices hushed. She took the stage and looked out at the faces. So many strangers, but many she knew. Fellow instructors and former classmates. Her own students, other local dancers and musicians. It gave her a warm and fuzzy feeling. She'd crawled into a hole after her father died that only deepened when her ex left her. She'd felt alone, and the fiasco with Derek had only made it worse.

But she wasn't alone. She could see that now. She had friends. She had Melanie. And if tonight was going as well as she thought it was, she was going to have her studio, too. One day, she'd have someone special again. Until then, this would be enough. And with so much support and encouragement around her, it was impossible to feel anything but love. And gratitude.

"Thank you for being here tonight," she said into the microphone, "for our Save the Shimmy Shop Benefit and Show. Like many of you, this is where I took my first belly dance class. Eight years ago, I walked into one of Almira's Tuesday night classes, and I never looked back. I owe so much to this studio. This is where I met Almira, my amazing mentor and friend. It's where I met my best friend, Melanie, who made tonight possible. And it's where I discovered how much I love belly dance.

"Last year, when Almira announced she would be retiring and planned to sell the studio, I knew I wasn't ready to say good-bye to this place—"

Derek's face in the doorway stopped her.

"It means everything to me," she continued, trying to focus, and trying to ignore his inscrutable expression. Why was he here? Why tonight? "You can't imagine how much it means to see that it means something to all of you, as well."

She couldn't think straight. She couldn't think at all. She searched for Melanie. For anyone. She could only see him.

"So, thank you for being here, and thank you for helping me keep this place going . . ."

A Belly Dance Diva peeked around the corner. The Divas! She had to remember to mention the Divas.

"We have many talented dancers performing tonight, including the amazing Belly Dance Divas.

But leading our lineup tonight is Janaya, a local dancer and one of our instructors, performing a tribal fusion choreography featuring an authentic Damascus steel saber."

The room erupted in applause and Abby left the stage as a lithe young woman with circus-colored dreadlocks appeared, carrying a curved sword in front of her like a ritual relic.

Instantly, Melanie was at Abby's elbow. "Are you all right? You looked a little rattled up there."

The words hardly registered. Abby searched the room for Derek, but he wasn't in the doorway anymore. He wasn't anywhere.

"Where'd he go?"

"Who?"

"Derek. He's here. Or he was." She thrust the microphone at Melanie. "I have to find him."

Before Melanie could stop her, Abby pushed her way through the crowd and into the hallway.

She spied him through the glass, standing under a parking lot light, talking on his phone.

She pushed her way out and waited for him to end his call.

"Definitely a go. Right. Metro section front page. Okay," he said into the receiver before ending the call.

"Look," she said, "I just want to say I'm sorry I barged in on your meeting. I know it was stupid, but you wouldn't take my calls and I had no other way to contact you. I'm so, so sorry and—"

He raised his hand to stop her torrent. "You don't have to apologize." He lifted a folder. The one she thought she'd lost.

"That's what I was trying to get to you. Before the meeting." She shook her head. The meeting that had already happened. "Before it was too late."

"Gladys found it, and it wasn't too late. You know, no one—not my father, not my uncles—had any idea my grandfather had amended the bylaws to give descendants the power to block sales and acquisitions. When I made it clear I intended to exercise that right, they decided to listen to my proposal."

His wide, satisfied smile loosened the grip on her chest.

"What was your proposal?" she asked.

"Well, you're looking at the new owner of the *Orange County Herald*."

"Really?" She could feel the joy radiating off him. She wanted so much to throw her arms around him, but she held back. "Congratulations," she said coolly. "I know how much it means to you."

"It means everything." He looked around, taking in the studio and the Shimmy Shop sign glowing red and orange against the night sky. "Like this studio apparently does to you."

She flushed, embarrassed that he'd witnessed that emotional moment on the stage. "I think I went a little overboard with my speech. I guess there's a reason I'm a dancer, not a public speaker."

"No, the speech was perfect," he said. He tugged at his tie like it was making him uncomfortable. "It was from the heart."

"Thanks," she said. It was so difficult being this close to him and not being able to touch him. If only she hadn't ruined everything. If only she had been honest. Maybe there would have been a chance.

No matter how hard she tried, she couldn't get past that thought. It was as if every nerve ending in her body was aware of him, from the citrus scent of his aftershave to the way his nostrils flared softly with each breath. Tonight he was more like the sweet, tender man she had known that first night. That amazing night that felt like a lifetime ago.

"Oh my God, Abby!"

Abby whirled around. Melanie was barreling through the studio door, waving the front page of the *Herald*. "Did you see this?" She stabbed her finger at the space above the fold reserved for the Friday Night Hot Pick. "It's us. The Hot Pick is us! That's why all these people are here. And there's a photographer here. Snapping the performers and the crowd. He asked me about you."

The puzzle pieces fell into place. Abby turned to Derek. "You did that, didn't you?"

He shrugged. "I figured it was the least I could do. It wasn't as much trouble as you went to for me, but, well, you look a lot better in a belly dance costume than I do."

That was a smile on his face. Definitely a smile.

"That's a matter of opinion," she said. "So is that why you came by tonight?"

"Mostly. A reporter who may or may not have been working on a personal matter for me pitched a story for tomorrow's paper that I wanted to check out for myself. Something about a local girl trying to save a beloved, but quirky, dance studio. I thought I'd come down and have a look."

"A story about the studio?" Something like that could bring in dozens of new students. It could turn the place around.

"I think it's a good story. Lots of possibilities. Place with a long, colorful history. Scrappy girl fighting against the odds. Following her heart." He paused and his head dipped closer to hers. "She is following her heart, isn't she?"

"I think that depends."

She could see her answer surprised him.

"Really?" he said. "On what?"

In a flash, she could see he wasn't as confident and self-assured as he wanted everyone to believe. He was vulnerable, just as she was, and in his way he was trying to reach out to her just as she wanted to reach out to him.

He wanted her, just as she wanted him.

All the harsh words and hurt feelings between them vanished as if they had never existed. All the mistakes and regrets. She forgot everything and said, "It depends on this." She laid her hands on his chest, rose up on her tiptoes, and kissed him. She filled it with all the longing and pent-up emotion, every feeling and desire she had suppressed since the day she had accepted his job offer. She surrendered everything in that kiss, and when she felt his arms entwine around her back, she knew he had surrendered, too.

A camera flash interrupted them. Out of nowhere a photographer was behind them.

"Sorry. I didn't know it was you, boss," the young man said when Derek whirled around.

"I'll expect that picture on my desk Monday morning," he said.

"Of course, boss," the man said, relieved. "She's all yours."

Abby wrapped her arms more tightly around Derek's neck and whispered in his ear, "She sure is."

***

Thank you for reading *Shimmy for Me.*

In the next book in the series, *Dance with Me*, Melanie wants to perform in the Belly Dance Divas' next world tour, and she's about to get her chance. The show's wild and sexy star drummer needs a pretend girlfriend to appease his family, and Melanie is happy to play along. But when her fake feelings turn real and threaten the arrangement, will she sacrifice her dreams or her heart? Learn more at http://www.DeAnnaCameron.com/book-two.

AUTHOR'S NOTE

Thank you for taking the time to read *Shimmy for Me*.

If you enjoyed it, please consider leaving a review at your favorite e-retailer or Goodreads.com. Your support makes a real difference and would be truly appreciated.

***

Have you read all the books in the *California Belly Dance Romance* series?

Shimmy for Me (Book 1)
Dance with Me (Book 2)
Another Dance (Book 3)
Jingly Bells (Book 4)

Visit www.DeAnnaCameron.com for details

ACKNOWLEDGMENTS

I'd like to thank some special people who contributed in important ways to this novella:

The Thursday crew and all the O.C. Writers who make time to support, motivate, and help each other.

Martha Trachtenberg and Anne Victory, for their keen editing eyes.

Sommer Stein, for the beautiful cover.

Kerri-Leigh Grady, for believing in this story, and virtually kicking my butt to finish it.

Novella Ninjas Janice Foy, Jennifer Savalli, Suz Jay, and R.J. Garside, as well as Tari Jewett, Liz Scott, Diane Becker, and Alane Canzone for their feedback and encouragement on early versions.

Austin and Chloe, for giving me my own happily-ever-after.

www.ingramcontent.com/pod-product-compliance
Lightning Source LLC
Chambersburg PA
CBHW020739130626
46554CB00006B/2065